THE FIVE MARYS

By Steve E. Upchurch

The Five Marys

Steve E. Upchurch, Author

Copyright © 2021 Steve E. Upchurch

Cover design by Logan Anderson

Book layout & design by Crystal Deeds

Paperback: 978-1-7345628-2-8
Nook: 978-1-7345628-3-5
Kindle: 978-1-7345628-4-2

Set in Bookman Old Style
Printed in the United States of America

All rights reserved. No part of this book may be reproduced in any form by any electronic or mechanical means including photocopying, recording, or information storage and retrieval without permission in writing from the author.

Requests for information should be communicated through the author's contact information below:
E-mail: Steveup93@hotmail.com
By calling or texting: 618-780-7564

The views of this book are solely the views of Steve E. Upchurch. Parts of some stories have been fictionalized for entertainment value.

All scripture references are taken from
the Holy Bible, New King James version
Copyright © 1982 by Thomas Nelson, Inc.

Table of Contents:

	Page#
Introduction:	I
Mary/Mother of Jesus	1
Chapter 1	3
Chapter 2	5
Chapter 3	9
Chapter 4	13
Chapter 5	19
Chapter 6	21
Chapter 7	31
Chapter 8	35
Chapter 9	43
Chapter 10	47
Chapter 11	53
Chapter 12	57
Chapter 13	61
Chapter 14	67
Chapter 15	69
Chapter 16	73
Chapter 17	77
Chapter 18	79
Chapter 19	83
Chapter 20	87
Chapter 21	89
Mary Magdalene	95
Chapter 22	97
Chapter 23	107
Chapter 24	111
Chapter 25	113
Chapter 26	123
Chapter 27	129
Chapter 28	141
Chapter 29	149
Mary/Sister of Lazarus	155
Chapter 30	157
Chapter 31	169
Chapter 32	179
Mary/James and Joses	183
Chapter 33	185
Chapter 34	187
Chapter 35	193
Chapter 36	195
Chapter 37	199
Chapter 38	205

Chapter 39 207
The Other Mary 211
Chapter 40 213
Chapter 41 217
Chapter 42 221
Chapter 43 225
Chapter 44 229
Chapter 45 235
Chapter 46 243
Chapter 47 253
Chapter 48 261
Chapter 49 263
Chapter 50 265
Chapter 51 267
Chapter 52 273
Chapter 53 275
Chapter 54 279
Chapter 55 291
Chapter 56 293
Epilogue 295
Acknowledgements 297

Introduction:

There are certain names, as soon as you hear them, you relate that name to a particular time period, or to a particular individual. If you are a baby boomer and you hear the name *Elvis*, you don't have to ask *"Elvis who?"* You know the person being referred to is Elvis Presley.

Some names are abandoned, never to be used again simply because one person with that name committed crimes so horrendous no mom or dad would ever think of naming their child by that name. For example, no one names their son *Judas* or *Hitler*, right?

The origin of the name *Mary* started in the Old Testament as *Miriam* and was later translated into Greek in the New Testament as *Maria*.

There were only two women in the entire Old Testament with the name Miriam. One was the sister of Moses, and the other was part of the lineage of Judah, mentioned in 1 Chronicles chapter four.

However, during the four-hundred-year time period between the end of the Old Testament and the start of the New Testament the name *Miriam/Maria/Mary* became quite popular. In fact, it became so popular there were at least five different *Marys* listed in the gospels that were part of the life and ministry of Jesus Christ.

Obviously, the most well-known *Mary*, was *The Virgin Mary*, the mother of Jesus Christ. Next was *Mary Magdalene,* (the only *Mary* whose last name is known), then there was *Mary* (the sister of Lazarus), then *Mary* the mother of James and Joses, and the *"Other" Mary* that shows up at the crucifixion.

Each *Mary* saw Jesus perform numerous miracles, yet

each one related to Jesus in different ways and have their own story to tell.

This story, while based on Biblical facts, is a fictitious story told from the viewpoint of Mary, the mother of Jesus.

MARY THE MOTHER OF JESUS

Matthew 1:
18 Now the birth of Jesus Christ was as follows: After His mother Mary was betrothed to Joseph, before they came together, she was found with child of the Holy Spirit.
19 Then Joseph her husband, being a just man, and not wanting to make her a public example, was minded to put her away secretly.
20 But while he thought about these things, behold, an angel of the Lord appeared to him in a dream, saying, "Joseph, son of David, do not be afraid to take to you Mary your wife, for that which is conceived in her is of the Holy Spirit.
21 And she will bring forth a Son, and you shall call His name Jesus, for He will save His people from their sins."
22 So all this was done that it might be fulfilled which was spoken by the Lord through the prophet, saying:
23 "Behold, the virgin shall be with child, and bear a Son, and they shall call His name Immanuel," which is translated, "God with us."
24 Then Joseph, being aroused from sleep, did as the angel of the Lord commanded him and took to him his wife,
25 and did not know her till she had brought forth her firstborn Son. And he called His name Jesus.

Luke 1:
26 Now in the sixth month the angel Gabriel was sent by God to a city of Galilee named Nazareth,
27 to a virgin betrothed to a man whose name was Joseph, of the house of David. The virgin's name was Mary.
28 And having come in, the angel said to her, "Rejoice, highly favored one, the Lord is with you; blessed are you among women!"
29 But when she saw him, she was troubled at his

saying, and considered what manner of greeting this was.
30 Then the angel said to her, "Do not be afraid, Mary, for you have found favor with God.
31 And behold, you will conceive in your womb and bring forth a Son, and shall call His name Jesus.
32 He will be great, and will be called the Son of the Highest; and the Lord God will give Him the throne of His father David.
33 And He will reign over the house of Jacob forever, and of His kingdom there will be no end."
34 Then Mary said to the angel, "How can this be, since I do not know a man?"
35 And the angel answered and said to her, "The Holy Spirit will come upon you, and the power of the Highest will overshadow you; therefore, also, that Holy One who is to be born will be called the Son of God.
36 Now indeed, Elizabeth your relative has also conceived a son in her old age; and this is now the sixth month for her who was called barren.
37 For with God nothing will be impossible."
38 Then Mary said, "Behold the maidservant of the Lord! Let it be to me according to your word." And the angel departed from her.

CHAPTER ONE

Why me?

I've asked that question over and over throughout my lifetime.

Why me? What was is about me, that I was chosen?

Let me introduce myself. My name is Mary. I am the mother of Jesus Christ, and do I ever have a story to tell you! In fact, it has been called *The Greatest Story Ever Told*.

Out of all of the people in the life of Jesus, I am the only one that was there when He was born, and there when He died. As His mother I was privileged to see Him in every stage of His life.

I'll never forget how entranced one of Jesus' disciples named Matthew was, when he sat down with me one day and began asking questions about how it all started. He spent several hours taking notes about the genealogy of Jesus and talking about the wise men that showed up shortly after Jesus was born. It became Matthew's favorite topic of discussion every time we got to spend some time together. Even though I also shared the part of the story concerning the shepherds with him, he was fascinated with the story of the Magi.

While Matthew connected with the Magi, Luke really seemed to connect with the shepherds.

But I'm getting ahead of myself. Let me start at the beginning.

Now, I'll warn you in advance ... there are parts of this

story you may find hard to believe. In fact, if I hadn't seen it with my own eyes, I would have a hard time believing it myself.

Even though I am now fifty-five years old, and several years have come and gone since I watched my son, Jesus, die at Golgotha, I can remember even the tiniest detail like it was yesterday.

I have pondered on what happened my entire life.

CHAPTER TWO

The first thing I want you to know is that I don't think of myself as special.

I was born and raised in the city of Nazareth, which is located about sixty miles north of Jerusalem. If you know anything about Nazareth you know that the people of Nazareth are considered to be some of the most common people around.

The population of Nazareth is only a little over four hundred people, so keeping a big secret was difficult. That was good when someone was in need, however it was not so good when someone was involved in something that may have been considered controversial.

I had a simple, yet wonderful, childhood. My mom and dad were great parents. My father's name was Joachim, and my mother's name was Anne, and I was the oldest of their 6 children.

My parents were common, but God-fearing people. My dad worked for a wealthy farmer on the northern side of nearby Sepphoris, the closest town of any size. My mom was a stay-at-home mom. She was never taught to read or write, so any education my siblings and I received came from our dad. Dad was unusually educated for what most people thought to be a simple farm hand. He absolutely loved teaching us kids what he had learned from his frequent visits to the nearby synagogue. He would sit for hours listening to the reading and teaching from the ancient scrolls of the writings of Moses and the prophets. Afterwards, he was always so excited to share with us what he had been taught.

Once when I was around ten years old, all of us kids were

sitting at the feet of my father after he had just returned from a trip to the synagogue. As always, he was excited to share what he had learned from the teachers and priests, but that night he was even more excited than normal.

He shared with us how the name *Nazareth* means "branch" in Hebrew. I remember beaming with pride, and thinking just how intelligent my dad was, as he excitedly explained that the name Nazareth came from the scripture where the prophet Isaiah wrote ... *"from Jesse's roots a branch will bear fruit."* (Isaiah 11:1)

"A branch from Jesse's roots? What does that mean?" I asked.

"Well, what is a branch and what is a root?" he asked me in return.

"The roots are the part that grows under the ground and supports the tree, and the branches are what grows out from the tree," I responded.

"Exactly! Wouldn't it be something if that scripture is talking about the coming of the Messiah," my dad answered, grinning in approval at my interest in the scriptures. "Wouldn't it be amazing if the prophet was letting us know that the Messiah's roots will be able to be traced all the way back to Jesse, King David's father, and possibly even our own little village of Nazareth?" he added.

"You do know who King David is, don't you?" he asked, looking at me.

My eyes twinkled because I knew that he was fully aware of how much I loved all of the stories about King David. Every Jewish child was taught the stories of the patriarchs of Israel like Abraham, Moses, David, and Elijah.

"Yes," I exclaimed. "David is the young man that killed

Goliath, that huge giant!"

"You are correct! And it's from King David that a branch will *bear fruit.*"

What my dad said sounded strange. Those words *"from Jesse's roots a branch will bear fruit"* seemed to stick in my mind. What did that really mean?

Little did I realize that this was the beginning of many prophetic things concerning the Messiah, especially those from the prophet Isaiah, that would unfold in my lifetime.

CHAPTER THREE

I'm sure I was like any other little girl when it came to babies.

When I turned six years old my mother took some old rags and made a toy baby for me for my birthday.

"What do you want? A baby boy or a baby girl?" she asked.

I didn't even hesitate. "I want a baby boy!"

"Okay, if you're sure that's what you want."

From that day on, I always hoped that when I finally did have my first child that it would indeed be a little boy.

I named the doll Benjamin, or *Benji* for short. I lugged that doll around with me everywhere I went until all that was left was a lump of worn-out rags. I really enjoyed acting like I was feeding him and changing his diapers.

As the oldest child it was expected that I would help my mom when my younger siblings came along. I didn't mind at all. In fact, I truly enjoyed it, and could hardly wait to have children of my own.

Then at the age of sixteen, my life took a drastic turn. A lot of my girlfriends, who were the same age I was, were getting married. Not me though, I wasn't really looking for a husband. In fact, I wasn't really interested in dating at all.

Then out of nowhere, I met the most wonderful man. I now know God sent him into my life. Even though he was several years older than I was, he was so kind and thoughtful I immediately fell deeply in love with him.

His name was Joseph, and he was in his mid-twenties. However, the age difference didn't bother me one bit. My dad liked him because he had already established himself as a skilled carpenter, and he treated me with great respect.

I knew my parents could tell things were getting serious between Joseph and myself when they sat me down one evening for a little talk.

"Joseph is a fine young man, and I have no doubt he would make a wonderful husband. Is that where this relationship is headed?" my dad asked, trying to use his fatherly voice of authority.

"Well, we sure do get along," I answered. "And I agree ... I think he would make a wonderful husband."

My mother moved in closer and looked me in the eyes. "Mary, if this is headed where we think it is headed, I'm sure you are starting to have feelings that you may have some questions about."

I felt my ears turn red. "Mom ... I already know about that stuff!"

"And just how do you know about that *stuff?*" she asked, with raised eyebrows.

"My friend's mom has already talked to her about it, and she told me."

I could see that both of my parents were quite relieved that they didn't have to talk to me about *that stuff.*

My dad stood and walked away quickly, however my mother hung onto my arm, letting me know that she wasn't done talking yet.

"Mary, the feelings that you are having are very natural," she said, almost in a whisper. "But I want to remind you of how very important it is that you keep your virginity until you are married."

"Oh Mom! I know that," I told her. "Anyway, he hasn't even asked me to marry him yet."

However, it turned out that my parents were right about Joseph's feelings toward me.

One evening while strolling through a local vineyard, and holding hands, Joseph and I began talking about our ancestors. Joseph was quick to tell me that he was a direct ancestor of King David. I could tell he was proud of his heritage.

"So, your great-great-great-great grandpa was the *infamous giant slayer*?" I asked, poking him in the ribs playfully.

"You got that right!" He responded, grabbing my hand, and holding me close. "And that same giant slayer blood flows through my veins!" he said emphatically.

I loved the passion I saw in his face and heard in his voice.

I didn't realize at that moment how Joseph being a direct descendent of King David would end up being part of prophetic scriptures being fulfilled in our lives.

Guiding me to a nearby hillside and sitting me down beneath a wonderful shade tree, Joseph knelt at my feet.

"Mary," he said, looking deep into my eyes, "I have something to ask you."

Could it be? Was this it?

"I love you more than I ever thought possible to love another human being. I see how wonderful you are with your siblings, and how honest and noble you are. Is there any way you would ever consider marrying me?"

I jumped into his arms so quickly I almost knocked him off his feet.

"Yes! Yes! A thousand times yes!!!"

CHAPTER FOUR

I was so excited to tell my parents and all of my relatives about our engagement, but I had one cousin in particular that I was the most anxious to tell. Her name was Elizabeth. She and Zechariah, her husband, were sixty years old. Even though there was a big difference in our ages we had become very close.

I drug Joseph to every relative I had in Nazareth, introducing him as my fiancé.

However, before I had a chance to share my great news with Elizabeth, an angel showed up in my bedroom one evening as I was getting ready for bed. I don't mean I had a 'dream' about an angel. I mean I was wide awake when Gabriel the Archangel showed up.

I don't mind telling you I was petrified!

Not knowing who or even what he was, the first thing I blurted out was ... "Who are you???"

"Gabriel," he answered.

"*The* Gabriel?"

He grinned. "Yes ... *the* Gabriel!"

"Gabriel the Archangel?"

"Yes, Gabriel the Archangel."

"The same Gabriel that appeared to Daniel?"

"Yes ... the same Gabriel that appeared to Daniel!"

I was so scared and in shock, I became speechless. Seeing that I had no more questions, he greeted me in the most unusual way. I'll never forget his words.

"Rejoice, Mary," he said, *"for you are highly favored. The Lord is with you, and you are blessed among all women!"*

"Huh?" was all I could get out.

"I can see that you are afraid," he continued, *"but you don't have to be. As I just said, you have found great favor with God."*

Then he said something that rocked my world.

"Rejoice, highly favored one, the Lord is with you, blessed are you among women!"

"Do not be afraid, Mary, for you have found favor with God. And behold, you will conceive in your womb and bring forth a Son, and shall call His name Jesus. He will be great, and will be called the Son of the Highest; and the Lord God will give Him the throne of His father David. And He will reign over the house of Jacob forever, and of His kingdom there will be no end."

"Huh?" I said again.

"Behold, you are going to conceive and bring forth a Son," he continued, *"and you shall call His name Jesus. And He will be great, and will be called the Son of the Highest. And the Lord God will give Him the throne of His father David. And He will reign over the house of Jacob forever, and of His kingdom there will be no end."* (Luke 1:28-33)

"Huh?" was all I could get out again.

I don't know how long I stood there speechless trying to make sense of what I had just been told.

Finally able to speak, I blurted out. "How in the world can that possibly be? I'm still a virgin!!!" My ears reddened at admitting something that personal to a complete stranger.

"*Relax, Mary,*" Gabriel replied, again with a slight grin on his face. "*The Holy Spirit will come upon you, and the power of the Highest will overshadow you, causing you to become pregnant.*"

Gabriel paused, allowing what he had just told me to sink in.

"*Oh, by the way,*" he added, "*that Holy One who is to be born will be called the Son of God.*"

"Okay ..." I answered. "And just when is this going to happen?"

"*So, you are willing to become the mother of the Son of God?*"

All I could do was shake my head up and down in acceptance of what just happened.

"*Then, as of this moment, you are now pregnant.*"

I remember standing there with my mouth hanging open ... trying my best to make sense of what I had just been told.

"*Oh, and one more thing,*" he added. "*Elizabeth, your cousin, has also conceived with a son in her old age. In fact, she is now in her sixth month.*"

Finally, I found my voice. "You have GOT TO BE KIDDING! I thought she wasn't able to have children!"

Then Gabriel did something I never expected. He threw back his head and laughed out loud!

"Well ... she's able to now!" he shouted.

I just couldn't believe it.

"You have got to be kidding!" I told him again. "That is impossible!"

"Nope. Not kidding. Mary, as you are going to see in your lifetime ... **with God nothing will be impossible**."

Talk about a true statement. I had no idea all the things I was going to witness in my lifetime, that, without God ... would have truly been impossible!

As quickly as Gabriel appeared, he disappeared, leaving me in a state of shock.

I don't mind telling you, I was very much overwhelmed!

I reached down and placed both my hands on my stomach.

"Am I a Mommy?" I asked myself out loud. "Am I really pregnant???"

Then I began to laugh.

At first it was more of a chuckle. Then it grew. Within a matter of seconds, I was laughing so hard, tears were streaming down my cheeks.

I am going to be a Mommy. I'm going to be a MOMMY!!!

Then, something Gabriel said suddenly clicked in my mind. Gabriel said, *"And the Lord God will give Him the throne of His father David."* (Luke 1:32)

There it was ... the name *David!* Joseph, my fiancé, was an ancestor of David!

I began to realize just how perfectly God's plan for my life was being revealed ... piece by piece.

And clearly Joseph was also going be part of the prophesies concerning the Messiah as well!

These were the first prophetic pieces of many that would fall into place over the next nine months.

CHAPTER FIVE

I sat there thinking ... *"God will give Him; this Son I am going to have ... God will give Him the throne of His father David!"*

My mind was swirling with all of the possibilities of who my son would be.

Suddenly it hit me.

JOSEPH!

What was Joseph going to say? Would he believe me? Would he still want to marry me???

And then I thought about my mom and dad.

MY DAD!!! OH, MY GOODNESS ... MY DAD!!!

How was I going to tell my mom and dad that I was PREGNANT? Especially after our little *talk*!

And what was that statement Gabriel made about my cousin Elizabeth? SHE IS PREGNANT TOO???

To say my mind was in a whirlwind would be putting it mildly.

CHAPTER SIX

I knew the first person I had to tell was Joseph.

I immediately went to Joseph's house, and thankfully he was home.

"Mary! What are you doing here?" he asked. "Are you okay? You look like you've seen a ghost or something. Are you sick?"

I blurted out, *"I'm pregnant!"*

It was as if the words were slowly penetrating his comprehension. At first there was absolutely no expression. He just stared at me, unflinching.

So, I repeated myself. *"Did you hear me? I said I'm pregnant."*

Without saying a word, he turned around and walked across the room and sat down in the first chair he came to.

I followed him inside and got down on my knees in front of him.

A little softer I said for the third time, *"Did you hear me? I said I am going to have a baby."*

Finally, he blinked. Then, he blinked again. The third time he blinked I saw his eyes starting to tear up.

"Did I just hear you right? Did you really say that you are *pregnant*?" he asked, pulling back from me as if he was revolted by my statement.

"*Yes, I'm pregnant,*" I repeated.
He exploded!

"How could you?" he screamed, jumping to his feet. **"How could you do such a thing?"**

Now his face was beet red and the veins in his neck were popping out.

"*Wait Joseph,*" I shouted back at him, trying to grab his arm. "*It's not what you think.*"

Yanking his arm from my grasp, he said in a strong, firm voice, **"I'll tell you what I am thinking. I am thinking if you are pregnant, you have been with another man. And if you have been with another man, the marriage is off!"**

Now tears were streaming down his face.

"*No, Joseph. It's not that way. Please stop and let me explain.*"

He slowly dropped his head and collapsed back into the chair.

"Don't worry Mary," he said softly, with his elbows on his knees, and his face in his hands. "I will put you away privately so that no one knows. Just answer one question for me."

"I'm happy to answer any question you may have."

"Who is the father?"

"The Holy Spirit," I told him.

He slowly looked up at me and squinted his eyes. Shaking his head slowly from side to side, he asked, "*The Holy*

Spirit? What in the world are you talking about? Are you drunk?"

I managed a small smile. "No, the Holy Spirit is the Father."

"Are you talking about the Spirit of God?"

"Yes."

"I'm not sure, but you might want to be careful with what you're saying. You just might be speaking blasphemy."

About an hour later, after telling him over and over how Gabriel had appeared to me, and how he told me I was going to give birth to the Son of God, Joseph finally stood up and said, "I'm sorry, Mary. This is a whole lot to absorb. I am going to have to think about this."

"I completely understand," I said as I turned and slowly walked out of his house.

I was in a complete daze as I made my way back home to my mom and dad's house.

But I was going from one dilemma to another.

How should I tell my mom and dad?

I decided to wait and tell them my story until the next morning. I was much too emotional and exhausted to face my parents at that moment.

Needless to say, sleep did not come easy. There were so many questions racing through my mind.

What if Joseph decided to end our engagement? Was it possible that God would want me to raise the Son of God as a single mother? What were my parents going to say?

What would my friends and relatives say?

Finally, I drifted off to sleep, only to dream of the worst possible outcome.

After a couple hours of restless sleep, I woke up the next morning early before the sun came up.

Again, all of those same questions were flooding my mind. Within myself I didn't have the answers.

If Joseph reacted that way, how in the world were my parents going to react?

I decided to try breaking the news a little gentler with them, rather than just blurting out *"I'm pregnant,"* like I did with Joseph.

However, as the first glimmers of daylight filtered through my bedroom window, I heard the sound of someone knocking gently on the window. I pulled back the curtain, and there stood Joseph!

I held my finger in front of my lips, giving him the *"be quiet"* sign, and pointed to the front door.

Complete panic set in. What if he was here to end our engagement?

I quickly put on a robe, pulled my hair back and tied a ribbon around it, and splashed some water on my face.

However, all it took was one look and I knew everything was alright with Joseph.

His countenance was absolutely glowing!

As soon as I opened the front door, he swooped me up off my feet and started dancing in circles.

"It happened to *ME*!" he shouted.

"Shhhh ... you're going to wake up the whole house," I said, not quite understanding what he meant.

"I can't be quiet. It happened to *ME*!" he shouted again.

"Okay ... *WHAT* happened to you?" I asked.

"An angel. I had my very own visit from an angel!"

"Seriously?"

"Yes, seriously!"

"Was it Gabriel?"

"I don't know. I didn't think to ask him his name."

"So, what did he tell you?" I asked excitedly. Now my voice was getting louder.

"Well, this angel showed up in my dreams last night, not in person like Gabriel appeared to you, but it was still very real!"

"So, what did he tell you?" I asked again.

"First, he called me by name. He said, 'Joseph, son of David, do not be afraid to take Mary as your wife. She has conceived, but it is from the Holy Spirit. She is going to give birth to a Son, and you are to give Him the name Jesus, for He shall save His people from their sins.'"
(Matthew 1:20-21)

"The angel told *YOU* the name of the baby?" I asked, placing a strong emphasis on the word "you", feeling just a twinge of jealousy.

"Yes. He was very clear about it. He said we were to name the Child, Jesus."

"So, now do you believe?"

"How could I NOT believe?"

My parents must have heard the commotion because I heard the sounds of them getting up.

Turning to Joseph I asked, "Are you ready to tell my mom and dad?"

A whole new look of panic covered his face.

I walked down to their bedroom and knocked on their door. "Mom, Dad, can you come out and talk for a few minutes?"

"Sure, Mary. Give us a minute to get dressed. We'll be right there," my mother answered sweetly.

I thought ... *boy am I ever getting ready to rock their world!*

Walking into the room my mother looked at me, then at Joseph.

"Joseph, what are you doing here so early in the morning?" she asked, rubbing the sleep from her eyes, and adjusting her hair on top of her head.

Then my dad made his way into the room, and rubbing his eyes he asked the same thing, "Joseph, what are you doing here?"

Then my mother turned back to me, looking closely in my face, and asked, "What's wrong, Mary? I can always tell when there is something wrong with you."

"Let's all sit down," I said, taking my dad by the hand and leading him to his favorite chair.

"Mom, can you sit on the floor by Dad?"

My mother followed and knelt on the floor beside my dad.

I pulled up another chair and, with Joseph standing behind me and his hands on my shoulders, I took a deep breath, smoothed the front of my robe, patted down my hair and looked up at both of my parents.

Not knowing for sure what to expect but realizing something was up, my dad began cracking his knuckles. Mom began chewing her fingernails.

Before I could speak my mom blurted out … "So, are you two still getting married? Is that what this is all about?"

I grinned a little bit, trying to relieve some of the tension.

"Don't just sit there … *say something*," she added.

"Yes, we're still getting married just like we planned."

In unison both parents breathed a sigh of relief.

"However, instead of waiting several months we are getting married right away."

I paused to see how they would take that news.

"Okayyyy …" my dad responded slowly, looking at my mother with a questionable look.

"And why the big hurry?"

I saw a scowl starting to appear across his forehead, as his eyebrows took a downward turn. My mom removed one finger from her mouth and began chewing on another.

I turned and looked at Joseph, hoping he would help me out with an explanation, but he just stood there with a blank look on his face. I realized I was going to have to explain what was happening on my own.

Remembering that I wanted to break the news in a gentler fashion than I did with Joseph, I asked, "Do you believe in angels?" looking from one parent to the other.

"Of course," they both responded at the same time.

"And do you believe that God speaks through angels?"

"Of course," they repeated.

Grabbing one of Joseph's hands and pulling him around to face my parents together, I said, "Well, the two of us have been visited by an angel."

I could see the confusion on both of their faces.

"At the same time?" my dad asked.

"No. Joseph saw his angel in a dream, while my angel visited me while I was wide awake."

Both parents edged forward in their seats.
"And ..." my mother said with a questioning tone.

"And each angel gave us the same message."

"Message?" my dad asked. "Are you going on a trip somewhere to deliver a message?"

Joseph finally found his voice. "No. The message was about Mary."

"Well …" I interrupted, "the message really involves both of us."

"Okay. Just spit it out. What is this *message* and what does it have to do with the two of you?" my dad said, starting to lose his patience.

"The angel informed both of us that I was going to get pregnant."

The same way it took some time for the message to sink in with Joseph, it was taking some time to sink in with my parents.

"Pregnant?" my mom asked.

"An angel told you that you are going to get pregnant?" my dad echoed.

"Yes. The angel said I was going to get pregnant."

Laughing out loud, my dad shouted out, "Why all the drama? That is *wonderful* news!"

"You mean we're going to be grandparents right away?" my mom asked, excitedly.

"Yes, Mom, you are going to be a grandma!"

"And I'm going to be a paw-paw?" my dad asked, grabbing my mom and doing a little dance in a circle.

I hesitated in breaking them up, not wanting to spoil the festive mood.

After giving them a moment of pure joy, I interrupted their happy dance. "Okay, sit back down you two. There is more to the story."

My dad completely ignored what I just said. "So did the angel say *when* you would get pregnant?"

"Well ..." I hesitated once more, "that's the *more to the story.*"

I couldn't wait any longer. **"I'm ALREADY pregnant!"** I blurted out.

It was like I threw cold water on the both of them. They both grabbed their mouths and my dad flopped down in his chair like a big bag of potatoes. My mother collapsed there beside him on the floor.

"What???" my dad shouted, looking at Joseph like he wanted to punch him.

Then my mother did something I did not see coming. She jumped up and SLAPPED ME!

My dad stood back up, and took a step toward Joseph. I could see the anger in his eyes.

"Joseph, I am so disappointed in you ...," he growled.

Then he turned to me. "Mary, how could you? Especially after we talked about this very thing!"

Joseph quickly moved behind me again, placing some distance between him and my dad.

Leaning his head over my shoulder, Joseph spoke up.

"It's not like that ... *I'm not the father!*"

CHAPTER SEVEN

Talk about mass confusion!

My dad's face was so red I thought his head was going to explode!

"What do you mean ... ***you're not the father?***"

Then my dad slowly turned and looked me square in the eyes.

"Mary ... what have you done! How could you?"

"My ... oh my ... what are we going to do?" my mom chimed in, barely able to speak.

I knew I had to jump in quickly.

"Wait a second," I shouted. "It's not like that! It's not like that one bit!"

Sweat was now pouring down my dad's beet-red face. "Are you pregnant, or not?"

"Yes, I'm pregnant."

"Is Joseph the father or not?"

"No, Joseph is not the father, but there's more to the story. Please ... sit down and let us explain."

They hesitated, but finally sat back down.

"The reason I asked if you believed in angels is because not only did the angel tell us that I was going to have a baby ... but he also told us that God was going to be the

Father!"

The look on my parent's faces was almost comical. It took a few seconds for what I had just said to sink in.

"Huh?" my dad muttered.
"Huh?" my mom repeated after him.

Slowly I began explaining how the angel told me that I would be moved on by the Holy Spirit of God and that in the process I would become pregnant.

"Huh?" my dad muttered again.
"Huh?" my mom repeated after him again.

"Yes. I am pregnant and not married yet. And yes, Joseph is not the father. But it's going to be okay. God is in control!"

Slowly the redness began to disappear from my dad's face and neck.

I watched to see how long it would take for my dad to realize what was happening.

He looked at me, raised his hand to his chin, and began rubbing his chin deep in thought. Then, slowly his eyes began getting bigger and bigger.

"You mean ..." his voice trailed off as he began to realize who his grandson was going to be.

"You mean ..."

My mom still hadn't caught on yet.

"What??? What are you two talking about?" she asked, looking back and forth from me to my dad.

My dad turned to my mom and said, ***"Our Grandson is going to be the Messiah!!!"***

CHAPTER EIGHT

I had a secret.

I had the secret that Gabriel told me concerning Elizabeth being pregnant.

No one else in our family knew. But I knew.

And I was keeping that secret.

I knew I just had to see her right away, so I quickly sent a message to her to see when would be a good time to visit.

I also included in the message that I had some exciting news to share with her.

She sent a message back right away, saying to come quickly, because she had some wonderful news as well.

I knew her good news ... about her being pregnant ...
She had no idea about any of my news!

The look on Elizabeth's face was priceless when she opened the door.

I didn't want to spoil her surprise so I let her speak first.

Her face was absolutely glowing! She was intentionally holding her stomach out as far as she could, with her fingers interlaced over her protruding belly.

"Can you believe it?" she shouted, bouncing up and down like a little school girl.

"I'm - going - to - have - a - baby!" she shouted, pausing between each word for the full effect.

She was absolutely radiant!

"Can you believe it?" she repeated. "Here I am ... sixty years old ... and pregnant!!!"

I hugged her as hard as I dared.

"Oh, my goodness!" she blurted out, quickly pulling away from me, and holding me at arm's length. "Did you feel that? It felt like little Johnny just did a backflip!"

"Little Johnny? Is that what his name is going to be?"

"Well, it's actually John. But for now, I am calling him Johnny.

"But did you FEEL THAT?" she continued. "Did you FEEL THAT, when we hugged?

"I just felt something ... I've never felt before."

I watched as tears quickly spilled down her cheeks.

"What was it?" I asked.

"It felt like the Holy Spirit of God just filled me from top to bottom," Elizabeth stated.

"Oh, that is so wonderful!" I exclaimed.

We embraced once again, feeling the awesome presence of God fill the room.

After a few minutes of basking in God's presence, Elizabeth invited me to sit down.

She poured us both a glass of water.

"Now ... how did this happen?" I asked, staring at her stomach.

"What???" Elizabeth replied, raising her eyebrows.

My face reddened ... "I mean ... obviously I know *how* it happened. What I mean is ... how were you *able* to get pregnant? I thought you weren't able to have children."

Once more the radiant look reappeared on her face.

"It's a miracle! And when I say miracle, I mean it was absolutely a God-sent-miracle."

"Six months ago," she continued, "Zacharias was praying in the temple, and an angel showed up and told him we were going to have a baby boy!"

"Where is Zacharias?" I interrupted. "I'd love to hear his story."

"Good luck with that. He doubted what the angel told him, so the angel struck him speechless!"

"Speechless? You mean he can't talk?"

"Not a peep!" Elizabeth replied, grinning from ear to ear. "The peace and quiet around here has been wonderful!"

"I am so very happy for you guys!" I replied, matching her grin for grin.

Suddenly Elizabeth grabbed me by the shoulders and held me at arm's length, and looking me square in the eyes, said, "Okay girlfriend, give it up. There's something different about you too!"

Before I could respond she opened her eyes as wide as she could get them and exclaimed, "He popped the question, didn't he? Joseph asked you to marry him!"

"Yes," I replied timidly.

She grabbed me this time and we did another happy dance.

When we finally stopped jumping, I just kept grinning at her.

"You mean there is MORE?" she asked.

"Yes," I responded, not quite sure how to tell her that I was pregnant too.

So, I just stared at her tummy and slowly interlaced my fingers and covered MY stomach, with MY eyebrows raised as high as possible.

"NO!!! Are you kidding me??? YOU??? You're pregnant, too???"

"Oh, that is WONDERFUL!" she continued. "So, when did you guys get married?"

"Last week," I told her quickly.

"How far along are you?"

"About a month," I answered.

Her smile was immediately evaporated.

"WHAT??? You HAD to get married???"

"Girl" she continued, "what were you thinking? Your dad is going to kill you!"

"Wait a second," I said, trying to cut her off, "it's not like that."

"What do you mean?" she replied, with her hands on her hips ... "it's not like that ... are you pregnant or not?"

"Yes, I'm pregnant, but it's not what you're thinking!"

Here we go again ... I thought. *The same 'it's not what you're thinking' conversation!*

"I'm thinking you and Joseph made a baby together."

"No ... that's not how it is ..."

"Well, then how IS IT???"

I could see that the situation was quickly getting out of control the same way it did with my mom and dad.

"Well ... it's rather hard to explain," I hesitated. **"Joseph isn't the father!"**

Why did I keep doing that same thing? I thought to myself. *I needed to find a better way to explain this.*

I thought Elizabeth's head was going to explode ...

"MARY!!! What have you done? Have you lost your mind?"

She looked at me with wide open, unblinking eyes.

Placing her hands on her hips she continued, with a critical sound in her voice. "Well, if Joseph isn't the father, then *who in the world is?*"

"It's odd that you would ask it that exact way. The Father isn't from this world."

Finally, Elizabeth was speechless. Her mouth opened ...

and closed ... opened and closed.

All she could do was stare at me with her mouth opening and closing, but no words were coming out. All she could get out was a grunt!

"Sit down," I told her, "Because you're not going to believe what I'm getting ready to tell you."

Then I told her how Gabriel appeared to me and told me not to be afraid, that I was highly favored among all women.

The color was slowly returning to Elizabeth's face.

"The angel said the Holy Spirit would move on me, and the Child inside of me would be called the Son of God," I told her.

"And that feeling you just had," I continued, "that feeling of the Holy Spirit ... I experienced that feeling too, only I could actually feel the Holy Spirit entering my Baby!"

Then it hit Elizabeth what this all meant. Slowly her eyes got bigger ... and bigger ... and bigger ...

"The MESSIAH!!! Mary ... you are going to give birth to the MESSIAH!!!" she shouted.

"I KNOW!" I shouted back at her.

Suddenly, that holy atmosphere entered the room once again. We felt the awesome presence of Almighty God, as we were overwhelmed by His favor that we felt over both of our lives.

I looked at Elizabeth, and she looked at me ... then a sacred hush fell over us.

I don't know how long we sat there holding hands, in the presence of the Holy Spirit. It was so overwhelming that neither one of us wanted to do anything ... other than soak it in.

Finally, Elizabeth spoke quietly. "So, what is the Messiah's name going to be?"

"Jesus," I answered reverently.

"Oh ... I love it!" Elizabeth whispered.

"Jesus ... Jesus ... Jesus ..." She whispered over and over.

"Oh yes, I love it very much!"

"And you are naming your baby John?" I asked.

"Yes. That is what the angel said we were to call him," Elizabeth answered.

"That's really something ..." I replied. "The angel that appeared to Joseph gave us the name Jesus."

"JOSEPH!" Elizabeth shouted.

"Oh, my goodness ... what does *Joseph* think about all of this???"

I laughed out loud, "Well ... it took a little while for him to come to grips with it all. But now he's totally on board!"

"And your DAD? Have you told your mom and dad yet? If so, how did your dad take it? I bet he about had a heart attack!"

I laughed, "Yes, it took a little while for him to wrap his mind around it all. But believe it or not, he and mom are actually looking forward to being grandparents to the

Messiah."

"So, what are your plans now?" Elizabeth asked. "With you beginning to show, the townspeople are going to put two and two together and realize you were pregnant before you and Joseph got married. Talk about a scandal ..."

"I don't know what to do. Do you have any suggestions?"

"I sure do," Elizabeth responded ... "You can stay here with us!"

And that is exactly what I did. I stayed with Elizabeth for three months, until she gave birth to John.

CHAPTER NINE

With her being as old as she was, I'll admit that I was really worried about Elizabeth giving birth. On top of that, this was going to be her first ... and only ... child.

However, when the day came, she delivered John without any problems or complications.

It was so funny ... the instant John was born, Zacharias' voice returned. He ran around the house hollering over and over ... *"I'm a daddy! I'm a daddy!"*

He was every bit as excited about being a father as any young man would be.

About a week or so after John's birth, Elizabeth and I went to the local synagogue. We had been talking about our sons and we were curious to see if the priest could show us some prophetic verses about the Messiah.

The priest was very helpful.

"There are actually quite a few verses that foretell of the coming Messiah," he told us. "However, one of the most challenging scriptures, at least for me personally, is found in the seventh chapter of Isaiah."

He paused to make sure he had our attention. "The scripture that challenges me the most is the one where Isaiah writes *'Therefore the Lord himself will give you a sign. The virgin will conceive and give birth to a Son, and will call Him Immanuel.'"* (Isaiah 7:14)

Elizabeth looked at me. I looked at her. We both grinned at each other.

"See what I mean about a challenging verse?" he asked.

With a look of disbelief on his face, he continued, "Imagine a virgin conceiving? How in the world is that going to happen?"

It was all I could do to not shout out ... *"IT'S ME!!! I'm that pregnant virgin!!!"*

It was also all we could do to maintain our composure.

Snickering slightly, Elizabeth asked, "Are there any other scriptures about the Messiah that intrigue you?"

"Yes. There's another wonderful passage in Isaiah about the Messiah," he replied. "In the ninth chapter it says, 'For unto us a Child is born, unto us a Son is given, and the government will be on His shoulders. And He will be called Wonderful Counselor, Mighty God, Everlasting Father, and Prince of Peace.'" (Isaiah 9:6)

Elizabeth whispered to me from behind her hand, "It sounds like your son is going to be a 'Prince.'"

We giggled at each other, at the thought of there being a prince in the family!

Then Elizabeth asked the priest one more question. "I'm just curious. Are there any prophecies about someone else that would be born around the same time as the Messiah?"

I knew she was curious about the miraculous birth of John.

"It's odd that you would ask that," the priest responded. "I was just reading in Isaiah the fortieth chapter about that very thing. Isaiah wrote that there will be a voice of one calling in the desert ... *'Prepare the way for the Lord!'*" (Isaiah 40:3)

"So, absolutely *yes*," he continued, "there *will* be a forerunner born before the Messiah!"

We were so excited we just turned and ran out of the Synagogue, leaving the priest without so much as a *Thank You*, or *Goodbye*!

Over the next couple of months, we talked a lot about the possibilities of our two sons, and thinking about the way they would change the world.

As soon as Elizabeth fully recovered from giving birth, I returned to Nazareth to be with Joseph.

When I left Elizabeth that day, I didn't realize that thirty years later her "Little Johnny" would baptize my Jesus as he declared, *"Behold the Lamb of God, who takes away the sins of the world!"* (John 1:29)

CHAPTER TEN

Joseph and I were so very happy.

I was so proud of how Joseph was handling our unusual circumstances. He was so attentive to every need that I had.

I knew that my stomach was going to get much bigger, but I wasn't expecting my ankles to swell the way they did. It was all I could do to get my sandals on my puffy feet. Joseph was so thoughtful as he went about massaging my aching feet every night.

Obviously, our marriage was not the typical marriage, however Joseph did everything he could to make it as normal as possible.

There was another area of our marriage where he showed great respect ... and that was our marriage bed. Out of respect to God and to me, and even though he had the right to do so, Joseph did not *know* me, in the Biblical sense, until after Jesus was born.

Just days before I was due to give birth, Joseph approached me with a worried look on his face.

"I have some bad news," he said. "We are going to have to take a trip to Jerusalem. Caesar Augustus has just signed a decree that everyone has to go to their home town and register."

"Everyone?" I asked.

"Yes. Everyone!" he replied.

"You have *got to be kidding!*" I told him.

I could not believe what I was hearing. Me, ready to deliver my baby boy, and traveling on a donkey for several days!

"I could go alone. Do you want to stay here?" Joseph asked me, with concern in his voice.

"Absolutely not!" I told him. "I am NOT having this baby without you by my side!"

"Okay ... then start packing up. We need to get on the road as soon as possible."

I'll never forget that time. There I was ... just a few days away from giving birth ... and we were getting ready to take a trip that was going to take at least a week ... if not longer.

"You do realize we're going to have this baby before we get back home, don't you?" I asked Joseph.

"Sounds like quite the adventure," he responded with a big smile.

Now ... I have a question for all the women out there reading this story.

Have you ever ridden a donkey?

Have you ever ridden a donkey ... non-stop ... for three or four days?

Or better yet, have you ever ridden a donkey ... non-stop ... for three or four days, while you are almost nine months pregnant?

If not, take my word for it ... donkeys are not the most comfortable riding animal there is.

Also, since I was only a few days away from giving birth, I was making trips to the bathroom every couple of hours.

Talk about UNCOMFORTABLE ...

On the third day we were only about four or five miles from Jerusalem when the labor pains started.

I turned to Joseph and told him as calmly as possible, so I wouldn't cause him to panic, "Joseph ... we are going to need to find a room as soon as we can ... Baby Jesus is going to be here shortly!"

It didn't work! Once Joseph realized what I was saying, he went into panic mode!

"Oh my ... oh my ..." Joseph began saying over and over, as he prodded the donkey to pick up the pace.

Sweat was pouring off his forehead, running down his cheeks and dripping off the tip of his beard.

"Oh my ... oh my ... oh my ..." he kept repeating.

"Are you okay?" he asked. "Do you want me to make the donkey go faster and risk bouncing you up and down more, or do you want me to go slower and take longer to get there? I don't know which is better!"

I'm sorry to admit I was *not* in the mood to answer those kinds of questions.

"I don't know," I snapped back at him. "Can you make the donkey go faster and smoother???"

Poor Joseph. He didn't know how to answer me.

Just when I thought I couldn't take it anymore we saw lights ahead.

"That is the little town of Bethlehem," Joseph told me. "If

I remember correctly, there's a small inn near here."

"I sure do hope so," I snarled at him, "because guess what ... my water just broke!"

Joseph's voice raised an octave ..., *"OH MY! OH MY! OH MY!"*

Once again, for all of you mothers out there, I want you to imagine yourself in labor ... your water just broke ... and the donkey you are riding on is now *trotting!!!*

"There it is ... there it is ... just hang on," Joseph shouted.

I was never so happy to see an inn in my life!

Joseph ran up to the front door, knocking frantically.

The most wonderful couple answered the door.

"We need a room and we need it NOW!" Joseph shouted loudly.

"We are so sorry," the inn keeper replied. "We just rented out the last room about an hour ago."

"Listen ... you don't understand," Joseph told him. "My wife is pregnant, and she is in labor *right now*. If we don't find some shelter, she is going to have this baby right here in your front yard!"

Turning and looking inside the inn, the man shouted out to his son and daughter, "Bartholomew, I need you to go clean out one of our stables as quickly as you can! Rebecca, go get a pail of clean water and as many clean cloths as you can find!"

As Joseph helped me down from the donkey and started gathering our belongings, Bartholomew ran ahead of us and quickly cleaned out a stable and threw some fresh hay on the floor. With his eyes wide open in amazement, he then stood off to one side as to not be in the way.

Rebecca, his sister, brought a large pail of water and a handful of white cloths and laid them nearby, and went and stood beside her brother.

Joseph quickly pulled a blanket from our belongings and spread it out over the hay, and gently helped me lay down on the blanket covered hay.

As the contractions grew closer together, Joseph turned to Bartholomew and Rebecca and asked them to close the door to the stable on their way out.

They took the hint and gave us some privacy.

Joseph was so protective and comforting. It made me fall deeper in love with him.

As the contractions got closer and closer, I remembered when one of my aunts gave birth. Her labor was so difficult her husband thought she may not live through it. I was worried that my labor might be that hard ... especially with this being my first child.

But it was like God took away almost all of the pain. Within a few minutes of settling into the blankets and hay, and to everyone's surprise ... Jesus made His grand appearance into this world!

It was WONDERFUL!!!

CHAPTER ELEVEN

I'll be honest with you ... I didn't know what to expect.

I knew that in a normal conception, infants usually have features from both parents.

I hadn't shared these thoughts with anyone, but I thought about this a lot. With God being the Father of Jesus, I couldn't help but wonder ... *would Jesus look "normal?"*

I mean ... think about it ... was there a chance of Jesus being abnormal?

I remembered talking to my dad once about angels, and asking what they looked like. That conversation led to us talking about how some believe that some of the giants that walked the earth early on, came from fallen angels having relations with earthly women.

If giants were a result of angels mating with earthly women, was there a possibility of Jesus being a giant?

Even though Gabriel didn't look abnormal to me when he told me I was going to become pregnant, I remembered my dad talking about the living creatures described by Ezekiel. They sounded pretty freaky to me, each one with four faces and four wings!

Was there any chance Jesus could be born with more than one face?

Would He have wings?

So, when Jesus came out looking like a normal baby, I was tremendously relieved.

That first night was so special.

There were a few people from the inn that heard a baby had been born, and wanted to stick their heads into the stable and congratulate us. We tried to be gracious.

Finally, the night grew silent and peaceful.

It seemed like all was right with the world!

Within a couple of hours of Jesus being born, He was ready to nurse for the first time. I can't find the words to express how I felt at that moment.

The King of Kings ... the Lord of Lords ... the Son of God ... the *Messiah* ... nursing for the first time.

It was surreal!

After Jesus' little tummy was full, and I had burped Him, the three of us lay there in the hay ... and once again I felt that same Presence that I felt when Jesus was filled with the Holy Spirit inside my womb.

It truly was a holy night!

I had smiled so much my jaws were aching ... but I still couldn't stop smiling.

Turning to me, Joseph whispered, "I just remembered another prophecy about the Messiah."

"Please tell me. I love hearing the words written so long ago about our child."

Joseph continued, "The prophet Micah wrote ... *'But you, Bethlehem Ephrathah, though you are little among the thousands of Judah, yet out of you shall come forth to Me the One to be Ruler in Israel, whose goings forth are from of old, from everlasting.'"* (Micah 5:2)

I remember looking at Joseph in awe.

"You mean to tell me it was prophesied that we would end up in THIS EXACT PLACE ... at THIS EXACT TIME ... to give birth to Jesus?"

A look of wonderful contentment was on Joseph's face. "Yes, that is exactly what I am telling you. Well, to be more accurate ... that is what Micah said!"

Then, there was another first.

Joseph looked at me ... and I looked at Joseph ...
And we both pinched our noses closed at the same time ...

"JESUS!!! What did You do???"

Yes ... I changed God's diaper!!!

CHAPTER TWELVE

We had no more got settled in and drifted off to sleep when we were awakened by a loud commotion outside the stable.

"But we just have to see Him!" someone was shouting. *"An angel sent us here ... to see and worship the Christ Child!"*

Hearing the words 'Christ Child,' Joseph quickly got up and went to see what was going on.

A couple of minutes later he returned, followed by several shepherds.

He must have seen the look of slight aggravation on my face, because he quickly said, "I know, dear. I know it's late. And I know you are exhausted, but you just *have* to hear what happened to these men ..."

"Please forgive us ma'am," the oldest looking shepherd spoke out. "But you're not going to believe what happened to us tonight!"

Seeing their excitement, I put aside my exhaustion, forced a smile on my face, and replied, "Okay ... tell me all about it."

They started out talking over each other so much Joseph finally stepped in and said, "Okay guys ... *one at a time!*"

They all turned and looked at the oldest shepherd, who began telling the story about how they were tending their sheep in a nearby field, when an angel suddenly appeared to them out of nowhere.

"And the glory of the Lord shone all around us!" the old

shepherd said, his eyes revealing how amazing it must have been.

The youngest shepherd blurted out ... "Yeh ... it nearly scared me half to death!"

"Hey ... *all* of us were terrified!" the old shepherd continued. "But the angel told us to 'not be afraid.' He said that tonight a Savior had been born in the town of David and that *'He is the Christ!'*"

"That is why we are here ... we are looking for the Christ Child!"

One of the other shepherds took over telling the story.

"The angel also said, 'Don't be afraid, for behold, I bring you good tidings of great joy which will be to all people.'" (Luke 2:10)

"Is the baby you are holding ..., is He really the Christ Child?"

Before Joseph or I could answer, the elderly shepherd interrupted with ... "The angel also said we would find a baby wrapped in swaddling clothes and lying in a manger. And here He is ... just like the angel said!" (Luke 2:7)

Finally, able to get a word in, I answered with a simple "*YES!*"

Instantly they all fell to their knees, bowed their faces to the ground, and began to worship Jesus!

I was moved beyond words, as these humble and backwards shepherds, raised their hands and their voices, reverently praising the Christ Child.

Little did I realize that what I was seeing at this moment,

would be repeated over and over, later in the life of Jesus.

In my lifetime I would see people from all ages and all backgrounds bow before Him and worship Him as the King of the Jews.

I don't mind telling you it was strange seeing people actually *worship* my Child!

After they finished worshiping Jesus, the shepherds gathered themselves together and told us the rest of the story.

They shared with us how a great company of heavenly hosts appeared in the heavens, praising God, and repeating, *"Glory to God in the highest ... and on earth peace and good will to all men!"* (Luke 2:14)

It was so heartwarming to see these lowly, hard-working men, who spent most of their time away from their families in order to provide for them, touched so deeply by their experience. It seemed like each shepherd was touched in their very own personal way, as each one told what they saw and felt.

One of the youngest shepherds looked me directly in the eyes and asked, "Mary, do *you* believe in angels? I mean ... I had heard stories about angels before tonight, but I wasn't for sure if they were really, real. Do *you* think they are real?"

I couldn't help but smile at the sincere look on the young man's face, as he was trying to make sense of what he had just experienced.

"Absolutely yes!" I responded, reaching out and patting the young shepherd's hand.

"Joseph and myself have both had a very real experience

with an angel. I also have a cousin that had an experience with an angel."

"You have? What was your experience like?"

All of the shepherds gathered around us, and sat cross legged on the hay as Joseph and I began telling how Gabriel had appeared to us.

"It was really Gabriel?" the young shepherd asked, wide eyed in amazement. "How did you know it was Gabriel?"

"He told me," I replied.

"Cool!" the young shepherd said, looking around at the other shepherds, and they nodded their heads in agreement. "Cool …."

We continued talking about the events that led up to this night, until eventually the elderly shepherd saw that I was getting exhausted, so he told the men to say their goodbyes.

I was deeply touched by how humbled they were by what they had seen and heard.

As they left, each one knelt before Jesus once more, bowing down to the ground, as they worshipped Him one last time. I noticed that every single one of them had tears streaming down their leathered cheeks as they reverently left the stable.

Joseph and I smiled at each other as we heard them making their way back to the fields and their sheep … still glorifying and magnifying God at the top of their voices!

CHAPTER THIRTEEN

A couple of days later, as we were getting our things together to make our way on into Jerusalem to register, we heard another commotion outside.

Once again, Joseph went to see what the clamor was all about.

When Joseph stuck his head back around the stable doorway, the look on his face was complete amazement.

"You will never guess who is here!" he said as he made his way to my side.

"I give up," I answered. "Who is it?"

"Magi!" he shouted. "There are several wise men from the East, and they're here to worship Jesus, just like the shepherds!"

"Take it easy Joseph, I'm not hard of hearing. You don't have to shout in my ears," I responded, pulling my head back and covering my ears with my hands.

"Oh, I'm sorry. But wait 'til you see these guys ..."

Before I could respond, one of the Magi stuck his head around the doorway and spoke, "Pardon me ma'am ... is now an acceptable time for us to see the Christ Child?"

"Sure," I told him. "Come on in."

Joseph was right. These men were very impressive. Their robes and garments were breathtakingly beautiful.

With our being from the small village of Nazareth, we had

only been around common folks with very little wealth. These men were wearing the most expensive garments I had ever seen. Their robes of scarlet and purple were decorated with gold and silver sewn into the fringes.

Then, the gifts they began pulling from the bags that they carried confirmed just how wealthy they really were. They began laying expensive gifts on the hay. There was gold, and frankincense, and myrrh.

I looked over at Joseph and his mouth was hanging wide open in amazement the same way mine was.

"What are we supposed to do with all of this?" I asked.

"These are gifts for the King," one of the Magi responded. "So, do whatever you wish with them. Keep them ... sell them ... we really don't care. We just want to honor the King."

And then ... just like the shepherds, they quickly fell to their knees and began to worship Jesus, bowing so low that their faces and long beards touched the hay that was on the stable floor.

I have to admit that some of the words that they used in their praise and worship were beyond my limited education, but there was no doubting their sincerity. I watched the tears flow and heard the emotion that muffled their words as they worshipped.

Rich ... poor ... educated ... uneducated ...

I was reminded of what the angel had told the shepherds. "I bring you good tidings of great joy which will be to all people!"

"ALL PEOPLE!"

Yes, in the years to come I would witness multitudes follow after Him, amazed at His words and miracles. My son, the Son of God, would minister to ALL people, regardless of their skin color, their background, their financial standing in the world, or how they dressed.

Once their time of worship was finished, the Magi sat down and told us the intriguing story about the star that appeared in the sky, and how they had been following that star for several months.

"How did you know to follow the star?" Joseph asked.

They looked at each other, shrugged their shoulders, and replied, "We don't really know. We just knew that the star had a special meaning."

They went on to tell us how as Magi, they studied a lot of different topics, including the constellations of the heavens, as well as the Old Testament scriptures and prophesies concerning the coming Messiah.

"So, when a new star suddenly appeared, we just *knew* it had to be a sign that the Messiah had been born."

"If you don't mind my asking," Joseph said, "how long have you guys been traveling, and what did your families think about you taking off on this odd journey?"

They all burst out laughing in unison.

"Well," one of the Magi answered, "we have been traveling for quite a while. We are from a part of Persia, that is about four hundred miles from here. However, it took us much longer because we could only travel after dark… since we were being guided by a star. And that star is currently stationed directly above where we are right now."

Joseph and I looked at each other with a quizzical look on

our faces.

Turning back to the wise men, Joseph asked, "You mean that if I go outside tonight and look up, I will see a star that is new in the heavens?"

"Absolutely," one of the Magi said, with a big grin. "As long as you know where to look!"

As we were contemplating the discussion about the star, one of the other Magi spoke up.

"As far as our families are concerned … yes, they think we are out on some wild goose chase!"

They all laughed at the remark.

I was still intrigued as to how they found the courage to set out on such an unknown and challenging journey.

"Is there anything in particular that helped you make the decision to embark on such a journey?" I asked.

"I'm sure you know the story of Abraham, and how he set off to find a land that God had promised to him, correct?" one of the Magi asked.

"Oh yes … we know that story very well!" I nodded.

Exchanging glances once more, the Magi continued. "Well, we found inspiration and direction from Abraham's example. If he could leave his homeland in search of a land whose builder and maker was God, we felt rather confident in leaving our homeland and following a new star that appeared out of nowhere."

That made sense to Joseph and myself.

"One more question, if you don't mind," Joseph asked. "We

noticed that you keep referring to our Jesus as a King. What's that all about?"

A frown curled the brow of one of the Magi.

"What's wrong?" Joseph asked.

"We have some bad news," he responded. "But let me answer your question first."

Looking lovingly down into the manger at Jesus he continued, "we haven't found any prophetic scriptures that tell us that Jesus will be a King, other than Isaiah writing that He will be the *Prince of Peace*. However, we know that the destiny of a Prince is to become a King. On our long journey here, as we talked about the Messiah, for some reason the word 'King' just seemed to fit. At least it did until we used that word while talking to King Herod."

As soon as he made that statement, we could tell there was more to the story because the countenance of each wise man fell. Then they shared the encounter they had with King Herod, and they warned us to be wary of him.

"We made the mistake of calling Jesus, the King of the Jews. And Herod was not happy at all with the concept of a 'King of The Jews' being born. So, beware, he may seek ways to harm the Child."

Yes, in my lifetime I would see thousands that *would* receive Jesus as King and Messiah. Multitudes would follow after Him. However, that day I realized there would also be thousands that *would not* receive Jesus as the Messiah!

Just as it was with the shepherds, we saw the reluctance of the Magi to leave Jesus. We were truly amazed at the looks of adoration that were on the faces of these highly educated and wealthy men as they humbled themselves in honest and sincere worship of a Baby that they saw as a King!

We thanked them for their generous gifts as they waved their goodbyes and started their long journey back to the east.

Our Son. The King!

CHAPTER FOURTEEN

Rather than return to Nazareth, Joseph and I heeded the advice from the Wise Men and spent the next several years in Egypt to escape any evil plots from King Herod.

Once again, Joseph pointed out another prophecy about the Messiah concerning our time in Egypt.

He said that Hosea prophesied ... *"And out of Egypt ... I called My Son."* (Hosea 11:1)

It was amazing to us, the things that seemingly just fell into place without us planning them in advance, that would end up being a fulfillment of prophecy. We did not search out prophetic scriptures, and then go out of our way to make sure that prophecy come true. All we did was live our normal lives, and follow the pathway that God was providing for us. Yet, right there in the middle of those decisions God was fulfilling prophecy after prophecy!

Shortly after we were settled in Egypt, we received a message that still haunts me to this day. We heard the news how King Herod, in his attempt to kill Jesus, set a decree that all baby boys, two years old or younger, were to be killed.

I was appalled at the thought!

My heart broke for all of those mothers and fathers, in and around Bethlehem, who had to bury their sons. All because of Herod's hatred for my son!

My heart broke for older brothers, and older sisters, that had to watch as their little brothers were ripped from their parent's arms, and were taken away to be slaughtered like innocent lambs.

Up to this point in time I hadn't quite made the connection between spotless lambs being sacrificed in the temple and Jesus becoming the Lamb of God that John the Baptist would speak about. But there was always this nagging, uneasy feeling in my heart about the long-term future of my son.

After we had been in Egypt for three years an angel appeared to Joseph in a dream, letting us know that King Herod was now dead. However, we were still uneasy about moving back to Bethlehem, so we moved back to Nazareth and settled into the life of a traditional Jewish family.

Joseph and I had several more children.

Having a greater appreciation for the scriptures, and knowing without a doubt the scriptures were true, we were very vigilant in teaching Jesus and His siblings the Scriptures.

CHAPTER FIFTEEN

When Jesus was two years old, His first half-brother, James, was born.

Jesus absolutely loved James. He loved playing with him and holding him.

And James loved Jesus.

As they got older, I watched as James tried to do everything that Jesus did. When Jesus climbed a tree, James was right there with Him, trying his best to climb as high as Jesus climbed.

When Jesus would challenge James to a race, I loved the look on James' face, as he tried his very hardest to keep up with Jesus. Every once in a while, Jesus would let James win, and when He did, it absolutely made James' day!

Out of all of His brothers, I could see that James was Jesus' favorite, even though if you were to ask Him, He would say He liked them all equally.

Then a year later came Joseph Junior. However, I began calling him *Joses*, to keep him from getting confused when I hollered for Joseph, his father.

Joses, like a lot of second or third born siblings, was quiet. He was a thinker, and I could see that Jesus really appreciated that about him.

He didn't try to compete with Jesus. The times he spent with Jesus were more about asking questions, or seeking Jesus' help when it came to his homework.

A year after that, along came Jesus' first little sister, Elizabeth. We named her after my cousin. She was a little spit-fire!

At this point Jesus was five years old, and as soon as Elizabeth was old enough to walk, she followed Jesus around like a little puppy dog.

More than once, Jesus would come in to where I was working, and ask, *"Mom, can you make Elizabeth leave Me alone?"*

Most of the time He would say that as a teasing way to aggravate His little sister, but there were times I think there was some truth to it as well.

A year and a half later, along came Simon. From day one he was the loudest of all of our children. If he didn't get his way, he would scream and cry like someone was beating the daylights out of him.

He was also the fighter. If anyone said or did anything to any of his siblings, including Jesus, he was ready to fight at the drop of a hat!

Then came the youngest sister, Rachel. She stole everyone's heart because for the first couple of years she was sick a lot.

Jesus, now eight years old, really took it hard. Every time she had a fever it was Jesus who was right there with her, wiping her forehead with a cool cloth. When she had a hard time going to sleep it was Jesus that would pick her up and rock her in the old rocking chair, singing softly to her until she was able to drift off to sleep.

I remember once, when she became deathly sick, and we really thought we might lose her, Jesus refused to leave her side. Even when I, as her mother, would try to get Him to let me take care of her, He would refuse. I would walk in to check on her, and there Jesus would be at her side, with His eyes closed, His head bowed, and I knew He was praying for her.

Then came our youngest son, Judas. As bad as I hate to say it, Judas was our problem child. As soon as he started putting sentences together, he began making up stories. Even if I caught him doing something red-handed, he would try his best to lie his way out of it.

Jesus was very troubled by Judas. When Judas was only three years old, and Jesus was fifteen, Jesus came to Joseph and myself and asked if he could talk to us privately.

We agreed, and as soon as we sat down, Jesus expressed His concern with Judas.

"There's just something about Judas that worries Me," Jesus said.

"If he's this much trouble at the age of three, what's he going to be like when he's, My age?"

We tried our best to reassure Jesus that first of all, Judas was *our* problem ... not His. And second, just because he was a problem child right now, it didn't mean he would be that way when he got older.

Fortunately, we were right about Judas.

In fact, after Jesus returned to heaven, every one of His siblings became devoted followers.

I am so proud of all my children, but I am especially proud of James. He is such a wonderful pastor in the church in Jerusalem. I know they didn't have the same Father, but I saw a lot of similarities in Jesus and James.

Sadly, James actually ended up becoming a martyr for the cause of his brother, Jesus. He was the second of my children to die. First, Jesus was crucified, and when James would not recant his faith in Jesus, he was taken to the pinnacle of the temple and thrown onto the cobblestone street below. Then he was beaten to death with a club.

However, his refusal to deny Jesus as the Messiah ended up leading a multitude of people to believe in Jesus!

Now, before I move on with the story, I want to clarify that Judas, the little brother of Jesus, is not the same Judas that betrayed Jesus.

However, I often wondered if Jesus could see a lot of similarities in the two of them and that was why Jesus chose Judas Iscariot to be one of His disciples.

I do know this. Having six younger siblings was a training ground of sorts for Jesus when He had twelve young men following after Him, looking to Him for guidance and counsel.

CHAPTER SIXTEEN

When Jesus was twelve years old, we caught another glimpse of how special He really was.

In trying to raise our children in the Jewish traditions of their forefathers, and in obedience to the commandments, we made the long journey every year to Jerusalem to observe one of our most holy feasts, the Feast of the Passover.

The Passover was a time when an innocent lamb was offered up for the sins of the nation. As Joseph and I studied the commandments and prophecies, anything to do with a sacrificial lamb now took on a greater importance to us. We began to understand that our sins, our transgressions, were being transferred onto the body of an innocent lamb, which would then be offered up on the altar, so that our sins would be pushed ahead in time, where they would be forever remitted by the Lamb of God.

As we slowly began understanding what this would mean for Jesus, the Passover became more meaningful ... and painful.

Our family had grown over the years, so the caravan to Jerusalem had become quite large. On this particular trip, on our way back home we didn't realize Jesus had stayed behind in Jerusalem until we decided it was time to settle in for the night.

I was quite anxious to talk to Jesus, and see what He thought of the Passover. However, He was nowhere to be found.

"Have you seen Jesus" I asked Joseph, with a slight panic in my voice.

"What?"

"I can't find Jesus. I've asked all of the kids, and they said they haven't seen Him all day."

Joseph grabbed my hand and we went from tent to tent, asking if anyone had seen Jesus.

Jesus was not to be found.

Panic was filling my mind.

"He must be back in Jerusalem somewhere! What are we going to do?"

Joseph rested a calming hand on my shoulder. "Don't worry. We'll find Him."

We let the rest of the family know to stay put, that we were going to rush back to Jerusalem and find Jesus.

I now feel sorry for the donkey I was riding. I beat that poor donkey mercilessly in my haste to get back to Jerusalem.

We spent the first day looking through the vast market places where food was sold. We doubled back and forth in the middle of the thousands of people that were still lingering in and around Jerusalem. No Jesus.

The next day we made our way to where the merchants were set up, that were selling their trinkets and jewelry. Again, we had to double back and forth to make sure we didn't miss Him. No Jesus.

Then, on the third day, it finally occurred to us ... the Temple!

Of course ... the Temple!

That had been the place Jesus was the most excited to see! And sure enough ... there He was.

We stood back for a few moments, watching in amazement, because there was a throng of people gathered around Jesus.

We listened as Jesus was asking very in-depth questions of the teachers. We could see that they were confounded, not only by the types of questions He was asking; but additionally, by the way He was answering their questions in return!

We were catching a glimpse of how Jesus would hold the attention of the multitudes, and how He would confound the Pharisees and Sadducees when they would try to trick Him into saying something they could use against Him.

However, ... Joseph and I were quite aggravated!

"Jesus," I asked Him, grabbing Him by the arm and dragging Him outside, "Do You have any idea of what You have put Your father and I through? We have been anxiously looking for You for three days! What were You thinking?"

I'll never forget the look on His face. I was watching a twelve-year-old Boy becoming a Man. For the first time I saw that He was beginning to fully understand who He was, and that He was on a mission from God."

I now shudder at His response.

"Why did you seek Me? Did you not know that I must be about My Father's business?"

"My Father's business?" I thought.

My first thought was ... "your father's business is being a

carpenter."

Then it hit me like a bolt of lightning. He was talking about His heavenly Father ... not Joseph!

That was the day that Joseph and I realized that we were not going to be able to treat Jesus like a normal twelve-year-old boy.

CHAPTER SEVENTEEN

The next eighteen years seemed to fly by.

However, as He grew up, I would frequently just sit and watch Him ... and wonder what God had planned for Him.

Joseph and I talked privately more than once about that very thing.

We spoke frequently about the ancient scriptures that foretold the wonderful things Jesus would do ... like preaching good tiding to the poor ... healing the brokenhearted ... proclaiming liberty to the captive ... opening prisons for those who are bound ... and comforting those that mourn. (Isaiah 61:1-2)

But it was also hard to ignore the scriptures that were also written about His death.

I really didn't like hearing those scriptures ...

For thirty years I pondered the things I had seen and heard in my heart.

CHAPTER EIGHTEEN

I was so very proud of Jesus. He was such a fine young Man. He was quiet, studious, and hard working.

I loved watching Him working beside Joseph in His teenage years as He learned the trade of being a carpenter.

"Measure twice and cut once" I heard Joseph tell Him on several occasions.

I was so amazed at the creativity that Jesus displayed when it came to working with wood.

It didn't take long for Jesus to begin making a name for Himself as a talented furniture designer and builder. He would spend countless hours, making sure every piece of furniture He built was exactly right.

Many years later I would read the words of those that knew Jesus, and marvel at how they saw Him as the Creator.

John would write how *"All things were made through Him, and without Him nothing was made that was made."* (John 1:3)

Paul would write, "For by Him all things were created, both in the heavens and on earth, visible and invisible, whether thrones or dominions or rulers or authorities—all things have been created through Him and for Him." (Colossians 1:16)

So, it made perfect sense that the mind of Jesus would be very creative.

I know that the first-born child is often seen as the favorite because the parents experience all of their "firsts" with that child.

The same was true with Jesus.

More than once, I heard Him called "Mama's Boy", especially from His four younger brothers: James, Joses, Jude, and Simon. Most of their teasing was good natured, but there were times I could sense a little bit of honesty and jealousy in their words.

Even His sisters would sometimes tease Him about being the favorite child.

I'll have to admit, it was difficult to *not see* Him as my favorite. Afterall, He was not only my first child, He was indeed, *special*!

He was also the only child that remained at home with Joseph and me. All of His siblings got married and left home by the time they were in their late teens. Not Jesus.

He never showed any interest in dating, or marriage.

But then, there were other things in which He showed no interest.

He saved every penny He earned. He simply was not interested in earthly things. While others His age were interested in investing in the purchase of livestock, or the latest robes or sandals, Jesus was satisfied with working hard as a carpenter and saving most of what He earned.

He asked me to keep His savings for Him, which I was glad to do. Later on, when He started traveling full-time, those savings came in very handy in providing for the needs of Him and the disciples.

Then came a sad day for our family. Joseph became very ill and died. I was so glad Jesus was still living at home. He was a great source of comfort.

However, I don't mind telling you that years later, when I saw Him raise people from the dead, I couldn't help but think back to the time when Joseph died.

I couldn't help but wonder ... what would have happened if Jesus had started His ministry sooner? Would He have healed Joseph? Would He have raised Joseph from the dead?

I did know this ... in the thirty years before Jesus began performing miracles there were a lot of people that *could* have benefited from His powers.

I still don't fully have the answer to that question as to why Jesus didn't start performing miracles sooner.

It may have had something to do with the laws of Rosh Hashana, the code of Jewish Law, that instructs congregations to seek certain qualities and follow certain guidelines when choosing a leader. One of those qualities is that he should be at least thirty years old.

Also, since Jesus was going to become a spiritual High Priest, according to the law a High Priest had to be thirty years old before being allowed to minister. (Numbers 4:3)

I finally had to come to terms with the fact that Jesus began His ministry when God inspired Him to do so. Period.

Another area of Jesus' life that I watched with great interest was His love life. His friends started dating, getting married and having kids. His younger siblings were getting married and having children. But Jesus never showed any interest in finding a wife or having children of His own.

Every time I would start to worry about those things, His words as a twelve-year-old boy in the temple would come back to me ... ***"Do you not know that I must be about My Father's business?"*** (Luke 2:49)

Still, 1 struggled with things a typical mother would struggle with, such as seeing her teenage boy turn into a young man, and then that young man reaching His late twenties and still living at home ...

CHAPTER NINETEEN

As Jesus' thirtieth birthday approached, I could sense an uneasiness in His demeanor. He was spending more and more time away from His carpenter shop, and more and more time in the synagogue.

One day He came bursting through the front door and I could see the excitement on His face.

"You'll never guess what happened to Me today," He exclaimed.

Before I could venture a guess, He blurted out, "I got baptized!".

"Baptized? How did that happen?" I asked, joining in His excitement.

"Well, I'm sure you've heard the news about John baptizing a lot of people ..."

"Yes. I've heard that he has drawn quite a following," I inserted. "But it's no wonder ... have You heard how he is dressing and acting?" I added with a grin.

Jesus returned my grin, "Yes ... he does look like a wild man ... eating nothing but locusts and wild honey."

"I know," I replied. "I heard he is wearing clothes he made from a camel's hide. Can you imagine? That has to be awfully rough on the skin!"

Jesus laughed out loud. "Yeh, that and the leather belt he is wearing is making quite the fashion statement!"

Both of us found the dress code of John to be quite

amusing.

"Is there any truth to the story that he actually called the Pharisees and Sadducees a bunch of snakes?" I asked.

Again, Jesus laughed out loud. "That's what I heard. I heard he called them a 'brood of vipers!'"

"I bet that didn't go over too well."

"Hey, they deserve it. Most of them are nothing but a bunch of hypocrites." Jesus added.

We were getting off the subject, so I redirected Jesus' attention. "So, continue with Your story about getting baptized," I said.

"Well, it had been a while since I had seen John. With the passing of Elizabeth and Zechariah I thought I would go see how he was doing."

I loved the excitement in Jesus' eyes.

"I heard he was down by the Jordan River, so I figured I would go check in with him. When he saw Me coming, he made quite the announcement. He pointed at Me and shouted out as loudly as he could, *"Behold! The Lamb of God who takes away the sin of the world!"* (John 1:30)

I don't mind telling you that when Jesus said this it took my breath away!

This was it! This was one of the things I had been pondering about the past thirty years!

Catching my breath, I asked, "So what happened next?"

"I just came right out and asked John to baptize Me. But when I did, John said that I should be the one baptizing him, not him baptizing Me."

"Why did You feel the need to be baptized? If You don't mind my asking," I asked, in curiosity.

"I just felt like it was fitting and proper. That I needed to do so to fulfill all righteousness." (Matthew 3:15)

I could see that this was something that Jesus was taking very seriously.

"Then what happened?"

"Aw, Mom, it was awesome! When I came up out of the water I looked up and the heavens opened and I saw the Spirit of God descending like a dove, and that Spirit landed on Me. At that same moment I heard a voice from heaven saying, *'This is My beloved Son, in whom I am well pleased!'*" (Matthew 3:17)

Once more my heart skipped a beat.

"Well, I guess that answers the question I had about why You felt like You needed to get baptized," I responded.

However, I couldn't help but continue with the question that I really wanted to know about.

"It also answers any questions or doubts You may have had concerning who Your *real* Father is, doesn't it?" I added.

"Does us talking about this make you uncomfortable?"

I hesitated. I had to admit that it *was* uncomfortable talking about when His siblings were present. But with Jesus one-on-one I was completely at ease.

"No," I responded. "Actually, You are the one person, other

than Joseph, that I am most comfortable talking with about it."

Even though I had told Jesus the story of His birth numerous times, I could see that He still took pleasure in hearing it again.

So once again, we talked in great length of His birth, the shepherds, and the wise men.

However, at that moment I sensed a shift had taken place in Jesus.

He completely abandoned His carpenter shop.

CHAPTER TWENTY

"Hey Mom, can you fix us something to eat?"

I looked up to see Jesus and four rather rough looking young men coming through the front door.

"Sure. But don't you think You should introduce Your new friends first?" I asked.

I could tell by the awful smell of fish that the they were fishermen.

Jesus smiled and responded, "Mom, this is Peter and his little brother, Andrew. This is James and his little brother John. They're all fishermen ... well ... they *were* fishermen. But now they are going to be *'fishers of men.'"* (Matthew 4:19)

Playfully, I reached up and pinched my nose ... "What is that awful smell?" I said, making a funny face at the four of them.

They all responded with a grin. "Yeh, we probably should have taken a bath before coming over!" Peter responded.

It was clear immediately that Peter was going to be the spokesman for the group.

We all had a good laugh.

"Fishers of men?" I asked. "What's that all about?"

Jesus smiled. "Well, My mission is to *catch people*. So, it only made sense to put it in terminology they understand."

"Ma'am, we're not quite sure what He is talking about. But we are all in!" Peter stated, with a big grin.

I told them to sit down while I put together something for them to eat, asking them to tell me about themselves.

We had a great time.

Yes, they were a little rough around the edges, especially Peter. But I could tell they were good men. I was happy they were going to be helping Jesus with His ministry.

After they left, Jesus and I sat at the dining table and continued talking.

"So, seriously, what was that *'fishers of men'* comment all about?" I asked.

A serious look now covered Jesus' face.

"Mom, I am starting to gather some men around Me to help Me in the mission I was sent here to accomplish. I am going to call them My *disciples*."

"And how many of these men are you planning on selecting?" I asked.

"Well, there are twelve tribes of Israel, so I think twelve would be the right amount. What do you think?"

"To be truthful, I wish Joseph was here for You to seek counsel from. But twelve sounds like a good number to me," I replied.

It seemed like every few days afterwards, Jesus was bringing more and more young men to meet me. We sat and had lunch together as Jesus began expounding to them about what His mission was going to be about.

CHAPTER TWENTY-ONE

Then came the wedding invitation.

Jesus and I received an invitation to the wedding of a young couple we knew in Canaan.

At that point, everywhere Jesus went His disciples were right there with Him. So, I told Jesus that His disciples could attend the wedding with us if they so wished.

I can't quite explain it. There was something stirring inside of me. It was like something was telling me that this day was going to be special.

The wedding was beautiful. We arrived in time for the wedding celebration, which lasted an entire day.

Then the following day, at the wedding feast, everything was going great until I overheard one of the servants in a panic, talking about how they were out of wine.

Something inside of me just said ... *"This is the time ..."*

I quietly went to Jesus, and took Him by the arm, pulling Him aside.

"Jesus, they are out of wine," I said to Him quietly.

Wrinkling His eyebrows, He pulled His arm from my grasp. "What does that have to do with Me?" He asked.

I didn't say a word, but I gave Him one of those looks a *mother* gives.

I grabbed His arm again, more firmly this time, and repeated myself. Only this time I looked Him right in the eye and said it more emphatically. *"Jesus, they are out of wine!"*

Then, leaning in so that only I could hear it, He whispered loudly right into my ear, *"I heard you the first time, Mother ... but My hour has not yet come!"*

I had thought about this moment for years.

But it was not my job to reveal who Jesus really was. I had made that decision long ago. There were so many times when other parents were bragging about their children, I was tempted to play the *"my kid is the Son of God"* card! But somehow, I had resisted.

Now, it was all I could do to keep my mouth shut. I know it was a silly thing ... running out of wine. And the answer was simple. Send someone to buy some more. Yet, there was this nagging feeling that would not go away.

I didn't challenge Jesus. I didn't scold Him. All I did was turn to the servants that were standing by. Pointing at Jesus I simply said, "whatever He tells you to do ... just do it!"

Jesus looked at me. I looked at Him. It was like He was waiting to see if I would back down. I refused to look away.

He didn't say it, but the look of resignation on His face reminded me of the times I had to correct Him as a child.

Quickly He turned to the servants and told them to go and fill the six large purification pots with water.

My chill bumps had chill bumps!

Was this it?

He didn't pray. He didn't wave His hand over the pots. He

simply dipped some of the water into a cup, gave it to one of the servants, and told him to take it to the master of the feast.

I about knocked people down that were in my way as I followed the servant with the cup of water in his hand, as he made his way to the master.

Jesus and the disciples were right behind me.

We all stood watching as the servant whispered something to the master and handed him the cup of water.

The master shook his head and said something back to the servant.

The servant then pointed to Jesus again, and repeated whatever it was he was trying to get the master to do.

Finally, the master shrugged his shoulders, and the look on his face said ... *I'm going to have to do this to get rid of this guy.*

Then, he took a sip from the cup.

I watched, slightly amused, as both of his eyebrows raised. He took another sip, and his eyebrows raised even higher. He took a third sip and then bellowed as loud as he could.

"This is the best wine I have ever tasted! Where did this come from?"

Once again, the servant pointed to Jesus!

Everyone turned and looked at Jesus, and I could tell by the look on His face He was not enjoying all of the attention He was suddenly getting. He quickly took a few steps backwards and tried to blend in with the crowd.

What ensued was a major rush of people running toward the six water pots to try out the new wine.

What also ensued was miracle after miracle, as Jesus began to *"be about His Father's business!"*

It was as if the floodgates were opened.

Immediately Jesus began traveling throughout Galilee, teaching in their synagogues, preaching the gospel of the kingdom, and healing all kinds of sicknesses and all kinds of diseases among the people.

As He did so, His fame went throughout all Syria. Everywhere He went they brought to Him all types of sick people who were afflicted with various diseases and torments. They also brought those who were demon-possessed, epileptics, and paralytics. And He healed them!

Naturally, great multitudes began to follow Him. There were people from Galilee, Decapolis, Jerusalem, Judea, and even people beyond the Jordan that became followers of Jesus. (Matthew 4:24-25)

It seemed like it was every other day or so that someone would stop by my house and update me on the latest miracle Jesus had performed.

My heart was overflowing. **Finally, Jesus was doing what He was born to do!**

After hearing so many stories, I decided to go see for myself. I packed up a few things and took a trip to go see for myself what Jesus was doing.

It took several days to track Him down. Not because no one knew anything about Him. It took several days because He was constantly on the move, going from city to city, and town to town.

I eventually caught up with Him.

I could tell He was pleasantly surprised to see me.

He was so busy we only had time to visit for a few minutes before the crowd around Him increased to the point that I needed to step back to allow those with needs to get closer to Jesus.

Then I saw *her* ... *Mary Magdalene.*

MARY MAGDALENE

Matthew 8:16 When evening had come, they brought to Him many who were demon-possessed. And He cast out the spirits with a word, and healed all who were sick,

Luke 8:1 Now it came to pass, afterward, that He went through every city and village, preaching and bringing the glad tidings of the kingdom of God. And the twelve were with Him, 2 and certain women who had been healed of evil spirits and infirmities—Mary called Magdalene, out of whom had come seven demons,

Mark 16:9 Now when He rose early on the first day of the week, He appeared first to Mary Magdalene, out of whom He had cast seven demons.

Note: The following is based on the assumption that according to church lore, Mary Magdalene may have also been a prostitute.

CHAPTER TWENTY-TWO

Mary Magdalene was about as opposite of Mary, the mother of Jesus, as anyone could possibly get.

Evil comes in many forms. It can be as simple as a sinful thought, or as extreme as demonic possession.

Unfortunately, with Mary Magdalene it ended up with demonic possession.

By the time she met Jesus for the first time, she was in her early twenties, and there were seven demons that had taken control of her life.

She could be acting and talking completely normal, but as soon as one of those demonic spirits took over her body, she would start saying and doing outlandish things that afterwards she didn't remember doing.

Her life was a life filled with extremes. Most of them were bad. She suffered extreme anxiety. She was filled constantly with extreme fear. She suffered with bouts of hate and anger. Eventually it reached a point where she had very little control.

This particular day was like any other day in the life of Mary Magdalene. Dealing with demonic spirits had become normal.

Little did she know, that as she woke up that morning, she would be a completely different person when she lay her head down to rest that night.

After a long and late night of another round of *entertaining*, she stumbled around the ran-down shack she called home. Her eyes were bleary, her throat was sore, and her head felt like someone was using it for a drum.

She finally gathered enough strength to wash her face, peering into the glazed over eyes that were looking back at her in the mirror. Deep, dark circles had formed beneath her eyes as she strained to focus on her reflection. The cold water felt good, but she knew that any good feeling she felt was short lived.

It was close to noon by the time she gathered enough strength and courage to head for the local market. Whoever the last man was that had been at her shack the night before had stolen all the food she had in her small cupboard.

Pulling her shawl down over her eyes served two purposes. The first was to keep the glaring sun from irritating her bloodshot eyes. The other was to hide her face from the judgmental stares of the other women of the village.

Just then, a young man went running past her, yelling at the top of his lungs, "Jesus is here! Jesus is here!"

"Jesus is here?" she asked herself. *"Who in the world is this Jesus person?"*

"Jesus is here! Jesus is here!" He continued shouting as he disappeared out of sight.

The young man's excitement stirred something inside of Mary.

Pulling her shawl up closer to her chin and tighter over her eyes, Mary grabbed the arm of a lady that appeared to be following the young man and asked, "who is this Jesus person?"

"Oh, you haven't heard? He's a healer and miracle worker," the lady answered with almost as much excitement in her voice as was in the voice of the shouting, young man.

"Miracle worker? You mean like a sooth-sayer or magician?" Mary asked, trying to stay in step with her.

"No," the lady responded. "From what I've heard He's some kind of teacher or prophet from God."

"So, what is so special about Him?" Mary asked, wincing as a ray of sunlight made its way past the hood of her cloak.

"I'm not really sure, but it sounds like everywhere He goes there are multitudes of people following Him and listening to His teachings."

"Are you going to go see Him?" the lady added.

Mary hesitated, and stopped walking.

Pulling her arm from Marys grasp and quickly hustling away, the woman added "That's where I'm going." Then, over her shoulder she added, "Maybe you should go see Him too!"

Mary Magdalene was intrigued.

"Maybe I'll go check this Miracle Worker out." Mary thought. *"What harm can it do?"*

Even though it took all of her strength, she finally caught up with the lady, and continued their conversation.

Out of breath Mary asked, "So, where is He and what is He doing now?"

"Do you know who Darius, the Centurion, is?" the lady asked.

"Sure. Everyone knows the Centurion."

"Well," the lady continued, "according to rumors, the Centurion's servant was so sick he was about to die, so the Centurion went and asked Jesus to heal the servant. Without even touching him, supposedly Jesus just spoke the word and the servant was healed!"

"The servant was about to die, and all Jesus did was say a few words and he was healed?"

"Instantly!" the lady responded.

"Does this Jesus person know how to cast magical spells?" Mary asked.

Sensing something sinister, and squinting her eyes, the lady slowed down slightly and looked closer at Mary.

"Do I know you?" she asked Mary. "You look familiar …"

"No," Mary responded quickly, pulling her shawl up over her nose so that only her eyes were visible.

"Anyway," the lady continued, "do you know Peter the fisherman?"

"Oh yes! Everyone in Capernaum knows old loud mouth Peter," Mary responded with a hidden grin on her face.

"Well, apparently Peter decided to become one of Jesus' disciples, and yesterday Jesus went to Peter's house to see Peter's mother-in-law, because from what I heard she was about to die too. However, according to eye-witnesses, all Jesus did was reach out and touch her hand and her fever immediately broke. They said that she felt so good, she immediately got up and fixed Jesus something to eat."

Now Mary was definitely intrigued.

Something inside of Mary was telling her to go check it out.

Within a matter of a couple of minutes Mary found herself in the middle of a crowd of people that were clearly on their way to see Jesus as well.

She kept her shawl wrapped around her face, and listened to the excitement that was in each conversation. The longer she walked and listened, the more her curiosity grew.

When they finally arrived where Jesus was, there was a huge throng of people gathered together. There in the middle of the crowd was Jesus.

Mary slowly made her way toward Him.

Not wanting to be noticed, she kept her shawl drawn tightly over her nose, leaving only her eyes exposed.

She took a few steps closer.

Jesus was speaking.

What was it about His voice?

She took a few more steps closer, without realizing her grip on her shawl was loosening.

Finally, she was close enough that she could see His face.

On one hand, she was touched by the overwhelming love and compassion in His eyes. But on the other hand, the closer she got to Jesus, the more unrest she began to feel in her spirit.

Then she knew. She could feel the darkness closing in. She knew that she was getting ready to have one of her demonic episodes.

"No! No! NO! ..." she thought to herself. *"Please ... not now. Not HERE ... in front of all these people ...!"*

She had lost count of the times in the past where she woke up, only to have people tell her that she had grown so violent and out of control they simply stayed clear of her until she settled down.

Most of the time she didn't remember what she did or said.

"Please ... not now," She thought to herself again, as the darkness now enveloped her consciousness ... *"Not here ... not in front of Jesus...!"*

Then everything went black.

When Mary opened her eyes, she was lying flat on her back.

"Where am I? What just happened?"

Jesus was kneeling at her side.

"Oh no! It had happened again!"

Quickly she tried to pull her shawl back over her face, but she couldn't find it.

Then she saw the outstretched hand of Jesus, reaching His hand down to help her up.

As soon as His hand touched her hand, a tingling sensation ran up her arm, all the way to her shoulder. However, His touch was different. It was not the same *touch* that she had felt from men in the past. This *touch* felt wonderful and wholesome.

"What happened?" she asked, looking into His eyes, as she struggled to her feet.

Jesus smiled, and calmly and quietly said, "I just cast seven demons out of you."

"What???"

His smile got a little bigger, as He leaned in a little closer, so that only she could hear Him. *"I said ... 'I just cast seven demons out of you,'"* He whispered.

Then she felt it. That darkness that had become her constant companion was gone! Gone was the hardness! Gone was the hatred and bitterness! Gone was the feeling of hopelessness!

Mary collapsed at His feet, as the tears of thankfulness began streaming down her cheeks.

"Thank You ... Thank You ... Thank You ...!" was all she could say.

Over and over, she just kept repeating it, "Thank You ... Thank You ... Thank You!"

Sensing that Mary did not want any further attention, Jesus simply turned, as several people approached Him, and He reached out and began healing them with His touch.

CLEAN! She felt CLEAN!

That dark spirit that was always there, waiting for the most inopportune time to show itself ... was GONE!

She slowly gathered herself and found her way to her feet

again. Backing away toward the middle of the crowd, but staying close enough to keep Jesus in her sight, she watched in amazement as He simply spoke a word to each person that was brought to Him. She watched as crippled limbs of one man were straightened! Another man that was clearly blind was healed instantly!

Mary was mesmerized. She could not get her feet to work. It was like they were frozen. She could not move. She *DIDN'T WANT* to move!

Then out of the corner of her eye Mary saw another man approaching Jesus, and instantly recognized the evil spirit that was in the man. He had the same demonic problem she had.

"What should I do?" She thought. "Should I try to warn Jesus?"

She recognized the darkness, anger and hatred that was in the man. She saw the evil that was pouring out of his eyes.

Walking quickly toward Jesus, the demonic, possessed man began to scream at the top of his lungs, *"Get out of here! ... Why are You tormenting us?"*

The crowd took a few steps back, until it was only the demonic possessed man and Jesus facing each other.

"Was this what just happened to me? Mary thought. *"Did I just do this same thing?"*

Without fear or a single word, Jesus reached out and touched the man.

Mary watched in complete wonder as she could actually *see* the evil spirits as they left the man.

"That very thing just happened to me!" she thought.
Then ... she stayed ... and she stayed ... and she stayed.

She could not leave. She didn't want to leave. It suddenly occurred to her that she had nothing to go back to.

So, she stayed!

CHAPTER TWENTY-THREE

I, as Jesus' mother, was there to witness the young lady with the shawl pulled up over her face as she slowly approached Jesus. I could tell by her actions that she was a deeply troubled and disturbed young lady.

She appeared to be in her mid-twenties, but there was a look about her that told me that she was much older in experience than she should be. I could also tell she had the potential to be a very beautiful woman, but her beauty was hidden beneath the dark and darting cold eyes of a very troubled young lady.

"Evil."

That was the first word that came to my mind when I saw her approaching Jesus. *"This woman is evil!"*

What was she going to do? Was she going to try to hurt Jesus? Was she there to be a disruption? A disturbance?

As she made her way to Jesus, it was as if there was a dark presence around her that caused people to move away from her. Quickly the throng of people that had gathered around Jesus began to part as she made her way to Him.

I saw some of the local women gasp, and the scowls of judgment that were on their faces as they began whispering to each other behind their hands.

"Mary Magdalene!" I heard one of them whisper loudly.

Another said, "It's that whore … it's that harlot….!"

Then I noticed how she was dressed.

Enticing. Provocative.

They were right. She was a prostitute! This evil woman *was* a prostitute!

I don't mind telling you my heart felt like it was going to pound through my chest.

I moved in closer, in case Jesus needed help from his mother. I was close enough to see their encounter firsthand.

Their eyes locked.

It was *hate* versus *love*!

It was *evil* coming against *goodness*!

It was *darkness* being confronted by *light*!

I'll never forget that moment when *His LIGHT* broke through *her DARKNESS*!

While others were backing away from her, Jesus walked toward her.

I don't know what Jesus said to her as He reached out and took her hands in His, but instantly her whole countenance changed as she fell unconscious at His feet.

When she opened her eyes, I was standing directly behind Jesus, and was close enough to see that her black, evil, eyes had turned into the most beautiful blue eyes I had ever seen!

Right before my eyes it appeared as if years and years of torment immediately disappeared from her face.

I was moved to tears as she fell at the feet of my Jesus, and she wept and wept, thanking Jesus over and over again.

Finally, Jesus reached down and helped her to her feet a second time, then turned to address other needs in the sea of people.

CHAPTER TWENTY-FOUR

It was one of those moments when a message is sent without the need for words.

I don't know why I thought I could hide in the crowd, and go unnoticed by Jesus.

Of course, He knew His mother was there!

As Jesus helped the young lady to her feet a second time, He turned His face toward me, and gave me that *look*.

He took her by her shoulders and turned her around, and ever so slightly pushed her my direction.

I nodded that His message was received.

Take care of her!

Little did I realize how much the life of Mary Magdalene would affect my life over the next several years to come.

I quickly made my way to her, and took her into my arms as she continued to weep.

From that day forward, we became the best of friends, and I became her adopted mother.

CHAPTER TWENTY-FIVE

"You are coming with me," I stated, as I took her by the arm.

"Who are you?" Mary Magdalene asked.

"My name is Mary. I'm the mother of Jesus, and you are coming to live with me for a while."

Turning her head and looking back at Jesus she asked, "*That* Jesus?"

I smiled. "Yes. *That* Jesus!"

"Oh, I have so many questions," she responded, grabbing my arm.

"And I can't wait to answer as many of your questions as I can," wrapping my fingers over the top of her hand.

When we got to my house, I told her that I would fix something for her to eat while she cleaned herself up.

As she sat down to eat, she exclaimed, "thank you so much. I don't know what I've done to deserve this, but I really, really appreciate it!"

"This is what being a follower of Jesus is all about," I told her.

"Then I definitely want to be a follower as well," she said.

I could sense that Mary Magdalene's story was going to take several days for her to tell, so I decided to let it unfold in its own time.

I started by asking simple questions that were easy to answer.

"How old are you?"

"I'm twenty-three."

"Do you have any siblings?"

"No. I am an only child."

"Do you have any hobbies?"

"No ... not really ..."

I could tell that she was hesitant to be forth coming, because she wasn't sure how well I would be able to handle the truth about her dark past.

But as we ate lunch, she slowly began to open up, trusting me enough to tell me her story.

"I was born out of wedlock to a woman named Delilah," she began bluntly, in between bites.

"My mother was a prostitute, and I never met, nor knew who my real father was."

She paused to take a drink, to see how I would react to her blunt admission.

Apparently, I passed the test because she took a deep breath and continued.

"My grandmother, Eunice, also lived with us in an old run down four-room house on the poor side of Jerusalem. While I was still just a child, I found out that my grandmother had also been a prostitute. However, by the time she reached her forties all my grandmother did was cook and clean the house."

"But," she added with a slight grin, "from the looks of the house, that didn't happen on a regular basis."

I grinned back at her.

"Obviously, my mother followed in my grandmother's footsteps. My mom once told me that she could barely remember the time of her innocence."

Mary paused again, looking into my eyes, waiting to see my reaction.

I hid my shock and simply nodded.

"I agree ... it appears your mother was simply following in her mother's footsteps."

Mary nodded in return. "Exactly. And the same thing happened to me."

I leaned in and patted her hand to let her know that it was okay ... she could tell her story without judgment from me.

Taking a deep breath, she started telling me her life's story.

"My earliest memories of my mother and grandmother revolved around chanting, the burning of incense, and praying to different spirits. There were always bottles of herbs and spices around the house, and a book of prayers that my grandmother had written. The prayers were written to idols and praying to the dead."

I concealed the shudder I felt on the inside. *Praying to the dead???*

"It was a common thing to smell the fragrance of incense

burning, and hear the sound of my mother and grandmother chanting their ritual prayers. However, they made it quite clear to me that I was not to discuss anything that went on in our house concerning their activities.

"'People will not understand' was what my mom repeatedly told me. *'They will think we are evil.'"*

Once more she paused, and looked into my eyes for approval to continue on.

"It's okay," I told her. "Go on … I'm listening."

She re-adjusted her position in her chair. "I didn't realize it at the time, but I guess what they were doing *was evil*. I realize now that they opened a door to a dark spirit world, and it not only affected them, it also affected me."

I nodded once again that it was okay to continue.

"The prayers, the chanting, and men coming and going at all hours of the night were normal."

"It was a generational curse," I inserted.

"What?"

"A generational curse," I repeated.

"What's that?"

"It's when a curse is passed down from one generation to the next."

Her face lit up. "That's exactly what was happening!"

She continued, "But like I said, my mom and grandmother reminded me over and over that I was not to discuss the activities that went on inside our home with anyone."

She paused ... "I know this may sound odd to you, Mary, but for me, all that stuff was just how it was. It was *normal*.

"But, as I grew older, I began to realize that the way we were living was not normal.

"First of all, most homes in our neighborhood had a mom *and dad*. Although those that lived around us were also poor, I noticed that the moms and dads in those homes had a trade or skill to make money. Some of them grew vegetables and traded them at the market for necessities. Others traveled into the wealthier sections of Jerusalem where they worked as servants or hired hands. However, my mother only *worked* after the sun went down."

I could tell that Mary was now getting more and more comfortable in telling me about how dysfunctional her upbringing had been.

"Even as a child," she continued, "I came to realize that what my mom did to make money was not socially acceptable ... that when men left our house after spending time alone with my mother, we suddenly had money for food and clothing.

"At the age of five years old, I had already become self-sufficient. I got myself out of bed every morning, fixed myself something to eat, and entertained myself until my mom and grandmother finally woke up from their late-night activities.

"One of my favorite times of the day was early in the morning, when it was still cool outside, and the sun was peeking over Mount Olivet. I loved how quiet and peaceful it was. It was during those times that I wondered about creation."

My heart ached for Mary.

"What do you know about creation?" I asked.

Mary smiled. "My friend Elizabeth, told me that God created the world."

"Who is Elizabeth?" I asked.

"Elizabeth was a little girl, the same age I was, that lived just a couple of houses down the street. Elizabeth said that her mom and dad took her and her siblings to the Temple every Sabbath. I loved it when she shared stories about what she was being taught in the Temple."

"What kind of stories?"

"Stories about a man named Noah, and how he built the ark. About men like Abraham, Isaac, and Jacob. I absolutely loved the story about the teenage boy named David that killed a giant with nothing but a sling and a stone."

I couldn't help myself.

"That boy named David ... was my husband's great, great, great, grandfather," I said with a smile.

"Really?"

"Really!"

Mary grew quiet, and slowly lowered her head.
"What's wrong?" I asked.

"I was just thinking about how wonderful it must be to know who your ancestors were. I don't even know who my father was," Mary responded.

Every time I thought I couldn't feel sorrier for Mary she

said something that took it to another level.

Pausing and looking around, Mary said, "I see that you live alone. Do you mind telling me what happened to your husband ... and what was his name?"

"His name was Joseph," I replied. "He was a wonderful, wonderful man. He died several years ago."

"Oh, I am so sorry," Mary said, reaching out to take my hands in hers.

Not wanting to get side tracked, I patted her hand and said, "One of these days I'll share my story with you, but for now I want to hear more about you and your friend Elizabeth."

She smiled and continued, "Well, I quickly found out that Elizabeth's parents didn't want her hanging around our house.

"'*Why don't you girls just stay here and play in our yard?*' they would say.

"To be honest with you, I preferred playing at their house. There was a different *feel* to their house. I can only describe it as good versus bad. Their house felt good, and our house felt bad."

"Do you know why their house felt *good* ... as you put it?" I asked.

Mary hesitated, not quite sure how to answer.

"I'll tell you why their house felt *good*," I told her. "It was because they believed in Jehovah God and served Him."

I could tell she was struggling to understand.

"This is one of those things we can talk about in the future," I said. "Keep going on with your story."

"Okay. As I was saying, I was exposed to the dark side of the spirit world at a very young age. The only prayers I heard at our house were prayers that were chanted to the devil, so I naturally gravitated that direction.

"By the time I was eight years old, I was praying to the dead every day and chanting the same prayers that I learned from my mother and grandmother."

I couldn't help myself ... I let out a huge gasp! The thought of an eight-year-old child praying to the dead shocked me.

Seeing my reaction, Mary asked, "Did I say something wrong?"

"No, dear. It's just the thought of an eight-year-old praying to the dead is hard for me to grasp," I responded.

I could see that she was at a point in her story where some of her memories were difficult, so I suggested that we take a break. I certainly needed one!

"I think we've talked enough for one night. How about we pick back up in the morning?"

Mary smiled at me, got up to her feet, walked around the table and stood in front of me.

"That sounds wonderful. Where do you want me to sleep? I can sleep on the floor ..."

"No need for that," I replied. "I have a spare bedroom, so you can just stay with me for a while. Is that okay with you?"

Mary smiled the biggest smile ever, and quickly gave me

the biggest hug. "Absolutely," she replied.

I couldn't help but hug her back.

As soon as I hugged her, she melted into my arms like a small child.

CHAPTER TWENTY-SIX

I let Mary sleep in the next morning.

While she was sleeping in, I went to the local market and picked up some decent clothes for her.

I had breakfast waiting for her when she finally made her way to the kitchen table.

"I'm so sorry," she exclaimed, rubbing her eyes as she sat down at the kitchen table. "That was the best night's sleep I have ever had! Your house has the same feel that Elizabeth's parents' house had."

"That's because we serve the same God," I replied with a smile.

"This is what I want," Mary responded, looking around.

"I want this for my family when I finally have one. To be honest, this is the first time I've even thought it might be possible. Until yesterday, the last thing I wanted to do was raise a child in the same environment I was raised in."

As soon as we finished eating breakfast, I could tell that Mary was ready to continue with her story.

But I had something to ask her first.

"Mary, it looks like we may be spending a lot of time together …"

As soon as I said that, Mary smiled the brightest smile and blurted out, "Oh I would *love* that!"

I smiled back at her. "With both of us being named Mary,

and your last name being Magdalene ... how about I call you Maggie?"

Her smile got even bigger.

"YES! YES! YES!" she shouted.

"Okay, from now on your nickname is going to be Maggie!" I told her.

She was beaming.

"A new name for my new life. I like that very much!"

"Okay, Miss Maggie, tell me more about your story," I said, anxious to hear more about from where Jesus had rescued her.

We settled into a more comfortable sitting area.

"I'll never forget the day when everything went from bad to worse," she started.

In my mind I thought, *how could it get much worse?* Sadly, I was about to find out.

Maggie took a deep breath and started.

"One day my mom said, 'Come on in here Mary. I have someone I want you to meet. Mary, this man's name is Saul. He going to be living with us for a little while.'"

Something inside of me cringed. Already I could tell her story was getting ready to get much worse.

She continued, "My mom stood next to Saul, with her arm wrapped in his, and she smiled a hopeful smile. 'Things are going to be so much better now,' she said."

"As she continued talking, Saul pulled his arm away from her and leaned down to look into my eyes. He had a big smile on his face, but instantly I didn't like him. He gave me a sleezy smile. I know his smile was designed to make me feel at ease, however, it made me feel exactly the opposite. An alarm went off inside of my head, telling me that this was not a good man. His smile could not disguise the disgusting glint of evil in his eyes. I was instantly uneasy being anywhere near him."

"Uh-oh," I said. I didn't like where this was going.

"However," Maggie continued, "that *'little while'* that my mom talked about, turned into several years. Saul became a permanent fixture in our home.

"For the first few years I think Saul could sense that I didn't care for him, so he kept his distance. However, when I was twelve years old, my body started changing."

Yes, I knew where this was going, and again I cringed.

Maggie continued, "In the beginning he was cautious to hide the looks he gave me when my mom was around. I noticed that his eyes would linger just a little too long on certain parts of my body. His eye contact would remain just a little too long when he looked into my eyes. I had a strange feeling there was always a silent question in his eyes. It was a question I did not like one bit!"

Maggie lowered her head, and also lowered her voice.

"Slowly, his smile and comments started taking on more of a flirtatious tone, if you know what I mean?"

I made a sad face and nodded.

"This went on for about a year. When I turned thirteen, my body matured even more, and Saul started getting even more brazen with his stares and off-colored comments.

"The first time he made a suggestive comment within earshot of my mother, I looked at her expecting that she would reprimand him and tell him to stop it. Instead, she acted like she was concentrating on the meal that was on the stove.

"Over the next several weeks his comments continued getting more and more brazen and sexual in content. Each time I would look to my mother, but she would pretend she didn't hear what he was saying.

"Then, he began standing too close. His hands would linger."

Maggie shuddered, as the horrible memories flooded her mind.

"His *breath!* Oh, his bad breath was awful.

"Repeatedly I looked to my mother for protection, and repeatedly she pretended not to notice.

"As strange as it may sound, I began to wonder. *'Maybe there's nothing wrong with this. Maybe this is okay. If my own mother is okay with it, maybe I should be okay with it as well.'*"

Now tears began flowing down Maggie's cheeks.

"I didn't realize that my mind was trying to make sense and justify something that was very, very, wrong," she sobbed.

I felt my face getting hot as I imagined the horror of the daily challenges Maggie had been exposed to.

Her head dropped, and she continued.

"My body revolted every time he brushed against me. I could feel the bile from my stomach filling my mouth every time he touched me."

As I listened to her story, I found myself wishing Saul was there in front of me so I could slap his face!

"Yet," Maggie continued, "there was still that part of my mind that wanted to believe it *had to be okay.*

"My mother, my protector, was allowing it ... *so it just had to be okay!*

"I did everything I could possibly do to keep from being alone with Saul. If my mom went to the market, I went with her. If she went to visit relatives or friends, I made sure to tag along."

Maggie's voice suddenly softened to the point I had to lean forward to hear what she was saying.

Her demeanor told me that she was getting ready to share something very, very painful.

Pain filled her eyes, and covered her face.

"Then came the morning that my mother went to the market while I was still in bed, asleep," Maggie said quietly. "I was left alone with Saul.

"I was startled from my sleep when he sat down on the edge of my bed."

Now her voice was quivering.

"In horror, and in an instant, my innocence was taken from me!"

CHAPTER TWENTY-SEVEN

Anger!

Anger was raging in my mind at the thought of this malicious man molesting a thirteen-year-old Maggie.

I'm ashamed to say that at that moment the protective mother in me rose to the surface and bubbled over.

Standing to my feet I demanded, "Where is he?"

"What?" asked Maggie, with a puzzled look on her face.

"Where is he? Where is Saul now?"

"Why?"

"I am going to go give him a piece of my mind!"

Maggie grinned slightly and responded, "You can't do that."

"Oh, yes I can! Where is he?" I demanded.

"Dead," was her blunt answer.

"What?" I asked with that same puzzled look now on my face.

"Yes. He's dead. At least that's what I heard."

I struggled with my emotions. I knew it was wrong to hate someone, but at the same time it was okay to hate the evil acts that someone may commit.

Maggie could see that I was struggling with what to say

next.

"It's okay," she said. "I'm just glad he's not able to do that to anyone else anymore."

I couldn't remember being this angry before. I wasn't quite sure how to handle it.

Sensing my uneasiness, Maggie quickly stood, ran to me, and began hugging me and saying, 'Thank you', over and over.

"What is that for?" I asked.

"I have never had anyone willing to defend me that way before," she said, her voice clouded with emotion.

Feeling like we needed a change of atmosphere I asked Maggie, "What do you think about us going to see if we can find out where Jesus is? If He's not too far away, maybe we can go see Him?"

It was the perfect distraction we both needed.

"Really? Oh, I love that idea! Let's go! Let's go right now!" Maggie shouted.

"Where is He?" she added.

"When I talked to Him yesterday, He told me that He thought He was heading toward the Sea of Galilee next."

Maggie was so excited at the possibility of seeing Jesus again.

Quickly I packed a few things for a trip, including food and water, and within the hour we were on our way.

Maggie was so excited ... it was like she was a little

schoolgirl!

"We're going to see Jesus ... we're going to see Jesus ..." she shouted out in a sing-song voice to everyone we met for the first thirty minutes.

I have to admit, her excitement was contagious!

Once we were on the road for a while, and both of our moods were better, I thought it might be okay to hear more of her story.

"So, did Saul molest you often?" I asked cautiously.

"Well, for the next couple of years, he was careful to only molest me when my mother was gone. I wanted desperately to tell my mother what was going on, but Saul told me that he would leave us if I told my mom. He made it very clear that if he left, my mother would have to start spending time with other men again to pay the bills. I knew what he meant, so I kept my mouth shut."

I was amazed at how she was able to make statements that carried so much magnitude, yet she made them as a matter of fact.

"In my heart," Maggie continued, "I knew that my mom had to know what Saul was doing. So, once again I convinced myself that if mom was okay with it, it must be okay."

"Oh, you poor child. Wasn't there anyone else you could go to?" I asked.

"No. The only relatives that I had were my mom and my grandmother. And it was pretty apparent that both of them were willing to live with what he was doing as long as Saul was paying the bills."

"This went on for a couple of years. Then, just a few weeks after I turned fifteen, I began getting sick every morning."

"No! ..." I exclaimed, clamping my hand over my mouth.

"Yes! I knew what that meant. It meant I was pregnant!" Maggie exclaimed.

"What did you do?" I asked, in amazement.

"I didn't know what to do," Maggie replied. "Should I tell my mother? Should I confront Saul? Should I just run away???"

"So, what *did* you do?"

"That evening I finally gathered enough courage to tell my mother."

"And how did that conversation go?" I asked.

"Not well at all. It could not have gone any worse. I asked her if she would come to my room so we could talk."

"'No' ... she told me. 'If you want to talk, you can do so right here in front of Saul.'"

"But I insisted," Maggie said, with a look of determination on her face. "I told her it was a conversation we needed to have in private."

"She finally consented, and followed me into my room. I could tell by the agitated look on her face that this was not going to go well."

"'What is it?' my mom asked impatiently. 'What is so important that you had to pull me away from my time with Saul?'"

"I told her, 'I'm sorry, Mom. But I have been getting sick every morning this past week.'"

"And how did she take that?" I asked.

"Oh, it was worse than awful. She knew immediately what I was insinuating. She demanded that I tell her who the culprit was.

"'So, you're pregnant, are you?' she screamed at me. 'How could you let this happen?'"

I was getting more upset by the second.

I blurted out to Maggie, "but *you* didn't *let* it happen! In actuality, *she* is the one that let it happen!"

"I know. And that's exactly what I told her," Maggie shouted back at me.

"Well ... good for you. I am so glad you stood up for yourself!" I shouted back.

We both had stopped walking and were looking fiercely at each other.

Then, we realized how loud we had gotten and burst out laughing at each other!

"Oh ... you poor child," I told her, as I took her in my arms again.

"So ... how did it end?" I asked.

"Awful!" Maggie exclaimed. "Instead of sympathy or concern, all I saw in my mother's eyes was a look of pure hatred!

"'Are you telling me what I think you're telling me?' my

mom screamed at me. 'And just who, pray tell, is the father of your little bastard?'"

I was speechless. I simply could not imagine any mother, no matter how bad of a mother she might be, treating her own flesh and blood this way.

Poor Maggie. She was so distraught, she collapsed to her knees there beside the road.

"Oh, you poor child ... you poor, poor, child," was all I could say, as I knelt there in the dust and held her close to me, rocking her back and forth in my arms.

Finally, Maggie gathered enough strength to get back to her feet and continue her story.

"Since my mom asked who the father was, I let her know. I told her exactly who the father was. 'It's SAUL!' I told her.

"Do you hear me ... *MOM???* It's your boyfriend!!!"

"Good for you!" I told her. "How did she take it?"

"She slapped me as hard as she could, right across my face.

"'Do you know what this means?' my mom screamed at me. 'You're going to mess everything up!'"

Stopping again, Maggie turned and looked into my eyes. "Oh, how I wish I could have had you as my mother!" she said, collapsing into my arms once again.

"I was devastated ... I felt so alone ..." she cried, burying her face into my shoulder.

We had made it to a large tree, with its limbs stretching out over the roadway, so I suggested we take a short break.

We sat down in the shade, and I opened my overnight bag and took out some water, gave her a drink, and poured some onto the hem of my robe and gently washed her face.

I don't know how long we sat there in the shade, but I didn't care. I was willing to stay as long as it took for Maggie to gather herself.

"While we have some nice shade, and this wonderful breeze, why don't we take a break and eat something for lunch?" I asked.

She nodded her head.

We slowly ate our lunch, as I intentionally moved the conversation in a different direction.

Eventually, that beautiful smile returned to Maggie's face.

"Are you ready to hit the road again?" I asked.

She nodded her head again.

I was really starting to admire this young lady. I could see the strength and resolve in her spirit that had allowed her to face such an awful tragedy at such an early age, and still somehow move forward.

"Let's do it," Maggie said, jumping to her feet, with a little more perkiness in her voice. "Each step we take is another step we get closer to seeing Jesus again!"

"That's the spirit!" I told her.

About twenty minutes after we had resumed walking, Maggie cleared her throat and said, "There's more to my story."

"I figured there was, dear. But you tell it when you are good and ready," I replied.

"As strange as it may sound," Maggie continued, "and as painful as it may be remembering it all ... it still feels good to finally be able to talk about it with someone ... someone that actually cares."

I smiled at her as she raised her head, in an act of determination, and continued her story.

"After slapping me, my mother stormed out of the room.

"Then my grandmother came into the room, in what was an attempt to console me. But I could tell by the way she was speaking that she was on my mother's side.

"So, with a broken heart I simply turned over in my bed and pretended to go to sleep."

She paused. "But Mary," she said, looking at me with great pain in her eyes, "I was so confused and afraid. 'Now what?', I thought. 'What was I going to do now?'"

Maggie continued, "After hours and hours of weeping and sobbing, I finally fell asleep. However, my sleep was interrupted with dreams of dark images. I felt like I was being consumed with pure evil."

I wanted to ask if that was when she became demon possessed, but I didn't want to interrupt her story.

"The next morning," Maggie continued, "my mother and grandmother came into my room with what Mom said was a glass of water. However, I noticed an odd smell and slight tint in color."

"Oh no! What was it?" I asked, with a worried look on my face.

"I asked them what it was, 'Never mind,' my mother said sternly. 'Just drink it. It's just water!'"

"'What is it?' I asked her again. I knew it wasn't *just water.*'"

"'Just do what I say', my mother told me. 'This will make our *little problem* go away!'"

I couldn't help but ask.

"So, did you drink it?"

"I was still hesitant," Maggie responded, "but I knew my mother was not going to go away until I did."

"I'll remember that look of evil on my mother's face until the day I die, as she thrust that glass into my hands. 'Go on,' she said, with a calloused voice. 'I've taken this so many times I've lost count.'"

Shivering, as if a winter cold had blown across her body, Maggie continued, "Reluctantly I raised the glass to my lips and with tears streaming down my face, and with a pleading look of *help me* on my face, I drank the potion that my mother had prepared.

"As soon as I finished, my mother snatched the glass from my hand and rushed out of my room as quickly as she could, all the while giving me a look that said, '*it was all your fault!*'"

In my mind I couldn't help but compare my first pregnancy with Jesus, to her first pregnancy.

My pregnancy with Jesus was scary, but it was also beautiful. Poor Maggie's pregnancy was filled with horror and gut-wrenching fear.

My first pregnancy was filled with hope, love, and fulfillment. Her first pregnancy was filled with no hope, no love, and no feeling of fulfillment.

Maggie continued. "Within a few minutes of drinking the potion I began to feel sick to my stomach. Once again, I was alone. Neither my mom, nor my grandmother, stayed with me.

"I felt so betrayed.

"First, I had been betrayed by this man that was supposed to be taking care of our family. Then I felt betrayed by my grandmother, who protected her daughter more than her granddaughter. And then, the greatest betrayal was my own mother ... the woman that had given birth to me and should have been my greatest protector!"

I could see that Maggie needed to get all of this out of her system, so I kept quiet and let her continue talking.

"That night, all alone, I had what would be the first of many miscarriages."

As soon as she made that statement, she immediately grew silent. I could tell that there was a whole lot of pain in that one sentence.

I thought about what she said, *'The first of many miscarriages ...'* This poor young lady had been carrying a burden ... she had been carrying so much guilt and shame ... I honestly don't know how she was able to do it.

A tear spilled down her cheek.

"That night" she continued, "not only did an infant die inside of me ... but a part of me died as well. Any innocence that might have still been there ... vanished. I felt that if I were going to survive, I was going to have to be as hard hearted as my mother was!

"So, I opened my heart and my mind, and embraced everything my mother and grandmother had taught me. Hey, the way I saw it was, if you can't beat 'em ... join 'em!"

"Oh Maggie! What did you mean by that statement?" I asked, almost afraid to hear her response.

"It seemed like there was no way out for me," she answered. "I felt like I was doomed to end up living the same life as my mother and grandmother."

"So how bad did it get?" I asked her.

"Real bad! Saul no longer hid his actions. His visits to my room became the normal."

"And there was nothing you could do about it?" I asked.

"Who was I going to go to? My very own mother and grandmother were condoning it. I had absolutely no one to go to."

Maggie paused. "I know I keep saying the same thing over and over, but it's true. Every time I thought it was as bad as it could get, I found myself in an even darker place.

"One night, Saul brought one of his so-called 'friends' to my room ... and my life as a prostitute began."

I was shocked. Not only by the brazenness of Saul, but also by the way Maggie could make this statement so matter-of-factly. The same way I might say something like "It's time to go to the market," Maggie had just blurted out, 'and my life as a prostitute began!'

Not noticing how much her statement shook me, Maggie

continued. "Yeh, after that, my mother showed me how to mix my own abortion potions. The next couple of years became a blur."

She continued on in her matter-of-fact tone. "Finally, at the age of seventeen, I grew tired of the abuse at the hands of Saul and his obnoxious friends, so I moved out on my own. I had no other skills, so I turned to the only thing I knew how to do ... prostitution."

As she paused in her story, I couldn't help but wonder how many other *"Maggie's"* there were out there. Broken ... abused ... used ... neglected ... with no one to turn to.

I made up my mind at that moment that I would take Maggie under my wings of protection and do everything I possibly could to bring about healing in her life.

CHAPTER TWENTY-EIGHT

Have you ever felt like God had put you in the right place at the right time?

That's exactly how I was feeling.

Had I not gone to see Jesus on the same day that Mary Magdalene showed up, what would have happened to her after Jesus cast those demonic spirits out of her? Would someone else have stepped up to help her. Or would she have been left on her own to try to work through the horrible nightmare of a past that was surely going to haunt her?

Yes. I was going to do my best to help this young lady any way I could.

As if she sensed what was going on in my mind Maggie asked, "Are you okay? I'm sure what I am telling you may be pretty shocking … I mean you were a virgin even after you got married … until Jesus was born … right?"

I grinned at her. "Yes. That is correct. Joseph and I weren't intimate until after Jesus had been born."

"So how many other children do you have, if you don't mind my asking?"

"Oh, I don't mind at all. Other than Jesus, there are four other sons, and two daughters."

It was nice to be talking about something other than Maggie's tragic stories for a few minutes. My mind was already on overload, and I sensed that it was about to get even worse!

"Yes," I continued, "The boys are named James, Joseph, Judas and Simon, and the girls are named Rachel and Rebecca."

"So, you named Joseph after your husband?"

"Yes. And he reminds me so much of his father. He is kind, compassionate, and loving. But ... that actually goes for all of my children," I said with a big smile.

"Can I ask another question?" Maggie asked.

"Sure. Ask anything you want," I responded.

"What do the other brothers and sisters think about Jesus?"

I hesitated. No one had ever asked me that question before. Maybe, just maybe, it was going to be good for me to be able to talk with someone like Maggie. With what she had been through, there were very few boundaries.

"Well ... that is a very difficult question," I confessed.

"Was Jesus your favorite???"

Yes. Mary Magdalene had a way of just cutting right to the chase!

Again, I responded, "That is a very difficult question!"

I paused, because I wanted to answer her questions truthfully, yet tactfully.

"Let me answer your last question first. Was ... or is ... Jesus my favorite?"

I took a deep breath, wiped my forehead and replied, "I have to start by saying Jesus *is* special. First of all, He is my first-born. I don't care what any parent may say, that first child is very special because you go through all of the 'firsts' with that child. Some of those firsts are wonderful, and some are not so much fun. The first steps ... wonderful. The first fever ... not so much. The first words ... wonderful. The first injury ... not so much. Is any of this making sense to you?"

Maggie's eyes sparkled. "Oh yes. It makes perfect sense.

"However," she continued. "It makes me long for my own child. And now, thanks to Jesus and to you ... that may be possible.

"But, that's not what I was really asking," she continued. "With what you have shared with me the last several days concerning Jesus being the Messiah, how could you *not* have treated Him differently than the other children? I think most people would understand if you did so."

It was time for brutal honesty.

Thankfully I felt more at ease having this conversation with Maggie than with anyone else I knew. With all that she had been through, and her brutal honesty with me concerning her past, I felt safe sharing some of my deepest and most sensitive feelings with her.

"Jesus *is* my favorite," I blurted out.

There it was! I had actually said it. I had been so afraid to even think it, that I had pushed the thought back into the farthest recesses of my mind, so as to not have to deal with it.

"I get it," Maggie responded. "Again, from what you have shared with me over the last couple of days, and according to the scriptures you have shared with me, aren't you supposed to love the Lord your God more than anyone or anything in the world?"

How was it that this young lady, so new in her faith in God, could cut through all of the *religious stuff* that sometimes gets in our way?

"Oh Maggie ... bless your heart. You just have a way of putting things! Yes, the scripture I shared with you the other day is one of the commandments that God gave to Moses. It says, *'You shall love the LORD your God with all your heart, with all your soul, and with all your strength.'* (Deuteronomy 6:5)

"Then with Him being the Son of God, aren't you commanded to love Jesus more than anything or anyone else?" Maggie questioned.

"There you go again ... making the complex so easy to understand," I smiled at her.

"Yes, I guess it is true that I am commanded to love Jesus in a special way," I continued.

"I do love my other children dearly, but with Jesus there is also a spiritual element to my love for Him. He is not only my son He is also my hope for salvation. Thank you so much for asking me such a hard question."

Smiling, Maggie said, "Oh, I love how you just said that! 'He is my son, but He is also my Hope!'"

"Well, He is! The same way He is the Hope for the entire world, He is also my individual Hope!"

Maggie smiled again. "But you still haven't answered my first question. What do your other children think about Jesus?"

That question pained me to answer. I paused and gathered

my thoughts before answering.

"I would be lying if I said it hasn't been difficult for them. I mean, when Jesus was born, we had angels showing up to announce His birth. We had shepherds showing up to bow down and worship Him. We had Magi showing up and showering Him with all kinds of expensive gifts and also bowing down and worshipping Him. Honestly, how could the birth of any of the other children even come close in comparison? His birth was so awesome and overwhelming, the births of all of the other children had no chance of even coming close in comparison."

I didn't realize it, but this admission had opened a door to a closet in my mind that I had never dealt with.

"I can see that this is very difficult for you to admit," Maggie stated. "But it also has to be nice to get some of this off of your chest."

"Yes, it really, really is. I have tried my best to not talk too much about it with Jesus' brothers and sisters. Because when I start remembering how awesome that night was, it's hard not to get super excited. So, I've always tried to be very cautious with them any time any discussion about His birth came up."

Again, Maggie asked the obvious question.

"So, do they believe? Do they believe that Jesus is only their *half-brother*? Do they believe that He is also the Messiah?"

Her bold question crushed me. "I know it may sound like I am dodging your question, but honestly, I don't know for sure. The same way I have tried to stay away from the subject, they have all done the same thing. They all *KNOW* ... but it's just something Joseph and I were always very cautious about when discussing it in front of them."

"Yeh, I get that," Maggie responded. "I'm sure having Jesus as an older brother could be very challenging!"

I could see that Maggie was still deep in thought. Finally, she just blurted out what was on her mind.

"Was Jesus *normal?*"

I laughed out loud, "Oh Maggie, I just love you to pieces. The answer to that question is 'yes' and 'no'. He was normal as far as a normal baby. He cried when He was hungry or had a dirty diaper ..."

Maggie couldn't help but interrupt ... "You actually changed the Messiah's dirty diaper, didn't you? You actually had to clean His dirty bottom ..."

We both burst out in laughter.

"Yes. Yes, I certainly did!" I answered, delighted at such wonderful memories of Jesus as a Baby.

I could see that Maggie's mind was swirling with other questions.

She began, "Did you ever have to spank Jesus?"
"Did He eat His vegetables?"
"How old was He when He learned to read?"
"How did He get along with other kids His age?"
I could see that this line of questioning could go on and on, so I cut her off.

"First of all, He was unbelievably intelligent. In fact, there were times we knew that He had knowledge that He could have only obtained supernaturally."

Maggie was very intrigued. "What do you mean by that?"

"There were times He would start talking about things just out of the blue that we knew He had not learned from us or from any of His teachers."

I then told Maggie about the time we traveled to Jerusalem for the Passover when Jesus was only twelve years old, and we didn't realize we had left Jesus in Jerusalem until we were on our way home. How, when we finally found Him, He was in the temple asking and answering questions with the temple teachers that left them completely astounded.

I couldn't help but laugh out loud at Maggie's expression. Her eyes and her mouth were wide open in intrigue.

She still wasn't done asking questions. "What about His personality? Was He outgoing, or was He the strong and silent type?"

"He was actually somewhat of an introvert," I started. "Now, don't get me wrong … from the time He was seven or eight years old, He could carry on a conversation with just about anyone. But He preferred spending time in the scriptures rather than being rowdy or playing games like most of the kids His own age."

Maggie leaned in and stared at me square in my eyes. "You have dodged the other question long enough. Do they believe? Do they believe that Jesus is only their half-brother, or do they believe that He is the Messiah?"

I could see that she was not going to give up on this discussion so I answered her the best I could. "Until Jesus started performing miracles just a few months ago, all they saw from Him was someone that was very knowledgeable about the scriptures and things of God. Other than that, He grew up pretty much a normal kid. I mean, He laughed at their silly jokes. He played with them. He complained about them when they bothered His stuff. They had their disagreements, just like any other brother would have with his siblings."

"Joseph and I tried our best to not cram the 'Jesus is the Messiah' message down their throats," I continued. "But it was something we felt like we could not ignore, so we did talk about it from time to time ... so, they *knew* ..."

"And now?" Maggie asked.

"And now ... they still prefer to not talk about it. So, I don't push the subject."

Conversation between us calmed as both of us were deep in thought.

Finally, Maggie broke the silence. "I don't have any siblings, so I don't have anything to compare it to, but it sounds like you and Joseph had a real challenge on your hands!"

"That's putting it mildly," I exclaimed!

CHAPTER TWENTY-NINE

I was surprised at how much that conversation drained me.

"Are you ready to stop and rest for a few minutes?" I asked.

Laughing, Maggie said that she was ready to take a break as well.

We had entered a small village, but their market place was vibrant with activity. We picked up some fresh fruit and bread and refilled our water bottles.

As we sat and refreshed ourselves, I held up my bottle of water and began telling her the story about how Jesus performed His first miracle by turning water into wine.

Once again Maggie came up with an off-the-wall question.

"Did Jesus dance at the wedding?"

I actually laughed out loud. The thought of Jesus dancing struck me so funny!

"Well ... did He?" Maggie repeated, with the biggest grin on her face.

"No ... He didn't dance."

Maggie continued with more questions about Jesus' personality. We have a great time talking about His likes and dislikes.

When we were refreshed, we hit the road again.

"Are you ready to tell me a little more about your life?" I

asked Maggie.

"Sure ..."

"Let's start by you telling me how you ended up in Capernaum."

Maggie took a deep breath.

"I moved to Capernaum, to get as far away from my mother, my grandmother, and Saul as I possibly could."

"That must have been very difficult."

"Oh, it was extremely difficult. Not only was I a new person in the neighborhood, but the only way I knew to support myself was by ... well ... you know what I was doing ..." she responded as her voice began trailing off.

"Then on top of that," she continued, "I never knew when I would have a demonic episode ..."

"Do you mind talking about that?" I asked.

"Well, it's not my favorite thing to talk about," Maggie responded. "But, what do you want to know?"

"I know you were exposed to evil at a very young age, but how old were you when you had, as you put it, your first 'demonic episode'?" I asked.

"I felt the presence of demons from an early age, but somehow I always found a way to resist them. However, when I was about fifteen years old, my mom and grandma were performing some of their prayer chants, and I joined in. I had repeated some of their chants with them before, but this time when I felt the presence of evil in the room, instead of resisting, I opened up my mind and body to it. Then, after the loss of my first child, I completely surrendered to the evil within me."

"So, what would happen when you had an episode?" I asked.

"I don't really know. I would black out and when I would come to, I would feel completely exhausted and mentally drained. I know I said it was okay to talk about, but if you don't mind, I really don't want to talk about that part of my life anymore."

"Of course," I replied. "I completely understand."

"So, where did you end up living in Capernaum?" I asked.

"Well, all I could afford was a single room shack that had been used by an old shepherd when he wasn't out in the fields with his sheep. It was awful. It smelled of wet hay, sheep urine and manure. But at least I no longer had to worry about Saul invading my room, abusing me, and taking all of my money.

"Word began to spread among the men that a new prostitute was available, and within a short time period I had all of the *business* I wanted.

"I quickly learned that there were men in the community that appeared to be upstanding leaders during the daytime, but when the sun went down their dark side came out. They began to frequent my shack on a regular basis.

"I was also becoming very hardened to the word 'love.' A lot of the men would tell me *'I love you'* in the middle of their lust. But their *'love'* was restricted to after hours, and in the darkness of the night."

My heart was touched by her openness.

"It must have been a very lonely life," I stated.

"Oh, yes! I was very lonely. Any considerations I had about the Creator God, that my friend Elizabeth told me about, evaporated quickly. I was living in a very dark and isolated place."

Then Maggie's face exploded in a huge smile.

"Then … thank God I met Jesus a few days ago and everything changed!"

We continued talking about Maggie putting her past behind her, and starting this new chapter in her life.

It was wonderful!

It was starting to get dark as we came near to the Sea of Galilee, so Maggie and I found a place to spend the night and turned in.

The next morning all we had to do to find Jesus was follow the crowd of people heading toward the Sea of Galilee. Everyone was talking about Jesus, the miracles He was performing, and His powerful teaching.

We arrived just as Jesus was starting to speak.

I loved how He took a simple story about sowing seed, and used it as an example concerning how different people receive the word of God, while others reject it. He also used a lamp as an example. He spoke eloquently about how the light of the lamp reveals things that have been concealed.

Maggie was completely in awe of His teachings. I could see that she was a changed woman. She was clearly disappointed when He finished teaching.

However, just as He always did, Jesus took time to

minister to the needs of the audience of people after He finished preaching.

We talked briefly with Jesus after He finished healing the sick, and then headed back home again.

I was glad we got to see Jesus again, but I also enjoyed the trip with Maggie because it allowed us more time together so we could learn more about each other.

From that time forward, Maggie became part of our family. In fact, several years later Maggie would become my daughter-in-law when she married my son, Joseph!

MARY THE SISTER OF LAZARUS

Luke 10:
38 Now it happened as they went that He entered a certain village; and a certain woman named Martha welcomed Him into her house.
39 And she had a sister called Mary, who also sat at Jesus' feet and heard His word.
40 But Martha was distracted with much serving, and she approached Him and said, "Lord, do You not care that my sister has left me to serve alone? Therefore, tell her to help me."
41 And Jesus answered and said to her, "Martha, Martha, you are worried and troubled about many things.
42 But one thing is needed, and Mary has chosen that good part, which will not be taken away from her."

John 11:2
It was that Mary who anointed the Lord with fragrant oil and wiped His feet with her hair, whose brother Lazarus was sick.

CHAPTER THIRTY

"Hey Mom!" Jesus shouted, as He entered my living room door. "You've got some company."

This had become a common thing. Jesus was always bringing people home, especially if they were in need of a home cooked meal or some motherly advice.

"Mom, this is one of my best friends, Lazarus, and his two sisters."

Lazarus grabbed me in a huge bearhug, literally lifting me off my feet, and he actually kissed me on the cheek.

Any objections I may have had were quickly dissolved by the huge smile on his face and his cheerful disposition.

"Oh Mary, I've heard so much about you," he said, sitting me back down on my feet, with his black curly hair falling down over his ears. His smile was made even brighter by the black curly beard that framed his face.

"It is an absolute honor to meet you," he continued, bowing slightly at his waist, as a sign of great respect. "Jesus has told us so much about you, we feel like we know you already."

"And this is Martha," Jesus interrupted. "You two should hit it off very well. She loves to cook the same way you do."

Martha had the same facial features as Lazarus, and the same black curly hair. However, I could tell she was rather shy and backward.

She stepped forward and shook my hand, and bowed slightly the same way Lazarus had bowed, honoring my position.

"And thissss ..." Jesus said, drawing out the *this,* as if He was introducing someone really special, "is Mary."

Laughing, He said, *"Mary ... meet Mary!"*

Mary had the identical bright smile of Lazarus. She also had the same bubbly personality.

"Oh Mary," she shouted as she grabbed me and literally jumped up and down, her curly black hair bouncing around her face. She was bumping into me so much she almost knocked me off my feet. However, she appeared oblivious to how much she had invaded my personal space.

I loved her immediately!

"I've been waiting to meet you since Jesus told us all about when, where, and especially *how* ... He was conceived and born!"

"He told you *everything*?" I asked.

"Yes, He told us everything! About the angels, how you conceived, about the shepherds and the wisemen ... everything!"

Just then Maggie, hearing the commotion, stuck her head around the corner, peering into the living room.

"Come on in, Maggie," I said.

"Jesus, do You remember Mary Magdalene?"

The brightest smile covered the face of Jesus. "It was wonderful seeing you the other day while I was teaching by the Sea of Galilee. I'm sorry I wasn't able to stay longer and talk with you."

Maggie's face lit up. "Oh, it's okay. I could see that You were very busy taking care of people. By the way, I loved Your sermon about how the Word of God is like seeds being sown, and how, as believers in Jehovah God, we should let our lights shine."

"You were listening," Jesus replied. "I like that!"

I could see that this conversation could go on for a while, so I interrupted to introduce Maggie to Lazarus, Martha, and Mary.

I noticed that the three of them were trying to figure out how Maggie fit into the picture.

Apparently, Maggie saw it as well, because she, just being herself, blurted out, "Hi! I used to be a prostitute and I was demon possessed!"

The reaction from Lazarus, Martha, and Mary was priceless.

Lazarus grinned.

Martha took a step backwards, placing her hand over her open mouth.

Mary rushed forward and immediately took both of Maggie's hands into her two hands!

"But Jesus set me free!" Maggie exclaimed. *"Jesus set me free!"*

I looked over at Jesus to see how He was responding. It truly was like His face was shining like the sun! His head was thrown back, His hair was bouncing, as He unapologetically laughed out loud. I'll never forget that sight.

Meanwhile, Mary had thrown her arms around Maggie, and was telling her how wonderful it was that Jesus had set her free.

I was so impressed with how openly Mary accepted Maggie for who she was, and who she had been.

Stepping forward, Jesus said, "Yes, Maggie, you look quite different than how you looked the first time I saw you!"

"Oh, Jesus! I owe You everything!" Maggie exclaimed. "My whole life has changed because of You! But I'm sure You hear that all the time!"

"Yes, I hear that quite a bit." Jesus replied. "But I still love hearing it!"

Still smiling, Jesus looked at me, then He looked at Mary Magdalene, and then to Mary, the sister of Lazarus.

"I was going to ask how we are going to keep three *Marys* from getting mixed up, but, Mom, it looks like you have taken care of part to the problem by giving Mary Magdalene the nickname *Maggie*."

Turning to Mary, the sister of Lazarus, He continued, "Since you are from Bethany, why don't we just call you *Mary B*?"

Mary's face broke into the biggest smile. "Okay! It's settled. I am now officially *Mary B*."

Looking at me she continued, "Since you are the original Mary, I think it's only fitting that we simply call you *Mary*."

"Sounds good to me," I responded.

Turning to Maggie, Mary B said, "Well, Maggie, it sure is a pleasure to meet you!"

"Well, everyone please find a place to sit, and I'll see if I can find something for us to eat," I said, happy to have a house full of people again.

Martha stepped forward, "I'd love to help, if you don't mind."

"Of course, I don't mind!" I spoke. "The more the merrier!"

As Martha and I were preparing the meal, we could overhear Jesus sharing more of His message with Lazarus, Maggie, and Mary B.

There were moments of silence, followed by moments of laughter.

Oh, how I wished it would always be this way. But, deep inside me, even in times like these, the feelings of pending pain and sorrow were never far away.

When the meal was ready, Martha and I served each one, and Jesus blessed the food.

Then, He shared the story of how He met Lazarus and his two sisters.

He told how He met the three siblings while He was working as a carpenter. Then He told their tragic story.

Their parents died tragically when they were mere teenagers, leaving them to practically raise themselves. That's why they were so close.

Mary B immediately took charge of the conversation, when it came to the part of the story of how they met Jesus.

"It was an ordinary day," she stated, not caring that she had a mouth full of food. I saw Martha roll her eyes and could tell it was all she could do to keep from correcting her little sister.

Wiping some of the crumbs from the corner of her mouth Mary B continued. "Martha and I were in the marketplace, buying some home supplies, when we heard a loud commotion. There were so many people, they were overflowing the street and pressing people up against the merchant tables that lined the market."

"'What's going on?' I asked one of the young ladies that was trying to push past me. I remember how she had on a bright yellow scarf.

"'It's Jesus of Nazareth,' the lady with the yellow scarf replied."

Without taking a breath Mary B continued, turning to each of us to make sure we were listening, "We had been hearing rumors about a man named Jesus, that supposedly was performing all kinds of miracles."

She then elbowed Jesus, who was sitting on the other side of her to make sure He was paying attention as well.

I could see that they had a great relationship. It reminded me of Jesus' relationship with His little sisters.

Mary B continued her story, "I wanted to know more about this *Jesus* person, so I asked the lady with the yellow scarf if she knew where Jesus was going to be.

"'He is supposed to be stopping at the edge of the city limits,' the scarf lady shouted over her shoulder, running down the street as quickly as she could go."

Mary B paused to take a quick drink of water and a quick

bite, but never stopped talking as crumbs fell from the corners of her mouth.

Again, Martha rolled her eyes. Only this time she could not help but speak up.

"Mary, please show some manners!" she said emphatically.

Mary B just laughed and continued on, completely ignoring her sister.

"Then I made the best decision on my life," Mary B said, lowering her voice and leaning forward.

I could see that she really enjoyed telling this story. I'm sure we were not the first ones to hear this same rendition of what happened that day.

Turning to Martha, Mary B said, "I told Martha, 'Let's go check this *Jesus person* out.'"

Mary B had finally sucked Martha in with her excitement, because now Martha's faced lit up, as well.

"Yes. That's exactly how it happened. I told Mary, 'Yeh, why not? We don't have anything else to do … let's go!'"

I looked over at Lazarus, and he winked at me. I could tell he was quite amused with both of his sisters.

Mary B didn't miss a beat.

"When we got to where Jesus was, I was mesmerized. I couldn't take my eyes off of Him. He was telling a story about a man that was going from Jerusalem to Jericho. But along the way he fell into the hands of some thieves."

Now Jesus spoke up.

"Mary B, I am impressed that you remember that story," Jesus said with a big smile on His face.

"Oh, I'll never forget that story, Jesus. You told how some thieves robbed the man and nearly beat him to death. Then, You told us how a priest came walking by, and when he saw the beaten man lying in the ditch, he moved to the other side of the road and just kept on walking, pretending he didn't see him."

The meal was now forgotten, as Mary B now had complete control of the conversation.

"I knew exactly what Jesus was talking about," Mary B continued. "I had witnessed that very thing numerous times. The local priests in Bethany seem to have very little compassion for the common people."

"Then a Levite came walking by," Mary B continued, "and saw the beaten man, and he too passed by on the other side of the road, ignoring the man's cries for help."

"Keep going, Mary B." Jesus inserted. "You're doing a great job."

She did.

Turning to Jesus, she said to Him, "What You said that day was so true concerning most of the Pharisees and Sadducees I had been around. I really didn't have too much use for them. They preach one thing, but do another. I was so glad that someone was finally bold enough to call them out on their hypocrisy. I loved it!"

We all smiled at Mary B's excitement.

"But I was also concerned. I remember telling Martha ... *'this Jesus guy had better be careful. If the leaders at our synagogue hear this, they are not going to be happy.'"*

Turning to Martha, Mary B asked, "And what did you say?"

Martha grinned. "I said *'I know. But I hope He keeps on telling it like it is!'"*

"So, who was it in My story that came walking down the road next?" Jesus asked, looking at Mary B.

"A Samaritan! Then a Samaritan came walking down that same road. But, when the Samaritan saw the beaten man, Jesus told us how he had great compassion on the beaten man. He bandaged up his wounds, placed him on his own donkey, took him to the nearest inn and took care of him."

Jesus grinned His approval at Mary B's recital, then questioned, "And why was that significant?"

Mary B hung her head slightly, and lowered her voice, "Because, as Jews, we don't really care much for Samaritans ..."

No one said anything for a few seconds. I could see that Jesus was intentionally letting the awkwardness hang there as a statement.

Then Jesus added, "And what did this good Samaritan do?"

Looking up through the dark curls that surrounded her face, Mary replied. "The good Samaritan gave the inn keeper two silver coins and told the inn keeper to look after the man. He told the inn keeper, 'If it costs more than these two silver coins, I'll reimburse you when I come back by.'"

Pausing and turning to Jesus, Mary B asked Him, "and what did You say next?"

"Do you think I don't remember what I said?" Jesus answered good naturedly.

"Oh, I know You remember what You said. I just want to hear You say it again!" Mary B responded, smiling boldly.

"I said, 'So, which of these three men do you think was a good neighbor to the man who fell among the thieves?'"

Mary B couldn't help but take control of the story once again.

"No one in that whole crowd said anything for a few seconds," Mary B stated, pausing for effect.

"Finally, one of the men from our village that claimed to be an expert in the law spoke up and said 'the one that had mercy on him.'"

Then Martha unexpectedly spoke up.

All eyes turned toward her.

"I'll never forget that moment," Martha said softly, with tears in the corners of her eyes. "Jesus, I remember how You slowly looked at each one of us in the crowd. It seemed like You paused when You saw Mary and me. Even though I knew You meant it for everyone, it was like You were speaking directly to us when You said, 'Go and do likewise!'"

It was finally quiet. No one spoke.

Clearly Jesus was allowing this message to sink in a second time.

Finally, Lazarus broke the silence.

Turning to Jesus, he said, "Jesus, Your story that day changed our lives. Mary and Martha came home that day and told me what they had witnessed. We decided that day that we wanted to be like that Good Samaritan. Now, we try to help anyone and everyone that we meet who has a need."

Jesus smiled. "I know you do. I am so very proud of you guys. That's why you are some of My dearest friends."

I was so proud of Jesus, my son. I could see that He was making a difference in people's lives everywhere He went. Not only were people being healed on the outside, but He was also making a difference on the inside.

His words and actions were changing the hearts of men and women for the better.

CHAPTER THIRTY-ONE

A couple of months later I heard a loud banging on my front door, only to hear the horrible news from one of our neighbors.

Lazarus was deathly sick!

"Come on Maggie, we need to get to Lazarus' house as soon as we can."

Bethany, where Lazarus lived, was only a few miles away, so we quickly packed up a few things and made our way there as quickly as possible.

As soon as Martha and Mary B saw me, they came running as quickly as they could. Both of them were crying so hard they could barely tell me how sick their brother was.

"So, what do you think is wrong with him?" I asked.

"We're not sure. He started complaining that his chest was hurting. Now he is so weak he can't even get out of bed," Martha explained.

"Have you let Jesus know what's going on?" I asked.

"Yes. We sent a messenger right away. The last we had heard Jesus was nearby in Jerusalem. So, we sent someone to find Him and tell Him to come quickly … that Lazarus was very, very sick," Martha explained.

Mary B interrupted. "The messenger returned and told us that he had found Jesus, and had given Him the message."

"Did the messenger tell Him that it was very urgent? That He needed to come quickly?" I asked.

"Yes. We made sure that He understood that Lazarus was deathly sick," Mary B responded. "So, He should be here any minute now."

I went in to see Lazarus, and I could tell by the coloring of his skin that something was terribly wrong with him.

"Hi Mary," he whispered. "I'm so glad that you came. Has anyone heard back from Jesus? Where is He? Does He know how sick I am?"

"Yes. Yes. And, yes," I answered. "A messenger found Him and let Him know that you are very sick. Just hang on, I'm sure He will be here as soon as He can. Just rest now and save your strength."

I have to admit that I was worried. One of my neighbors had the same symptoms, so I knew that Lazarus' heart was failing him. He didn't have long to live.

We waited.

And we waited.

Still ... no Jesus.

We paced back and forth.

We prayed.

Still ... no Jesus.

I finally went out and searched until I found the messenger.

"Are you SURE ... you told Jesus how important it was that He come quickly?" I asked him, grabbing him by the shoulders, and looking him square in the eyes.

"Yes," he replied. "I told Him that He needed to come quickly, that Lazarus was about to die!"

"And you're sure He's only a short journey from here?"

"Yes! I don't know what else to tell you. Go find Him yourself if you don't believe me!"

We waited ... and waited ... but Jesus never showed up.

All I could think of, as to why Jesus hadn't showed up yet, was there was an emergency somewhere else, where He was needed.

Then the unthinkable happened. Lazarus died.

Martha and Mary were devastated!

I couldn't believe it. How could Jesus NOT have come?

Especially since He was only a short distance away ...

I went and found the messenger again, and told him to go and try to find Jesus again and let Him know that Lazarus was now dead. That He needed to get here right away.

Several hours later the messenger returned. He said that he had found Jesus and had delivered the message.

"Did He say why He wasn't here yet?" I asked, with a hint of aggravation showing in my voice.

The messenger just shook his head, and said, "No ma'am. All He did was thank me for getting the message to him."

I was so confused. Mary and Martha were so confused. Maggie was so confused.

What was Jesus thinking?

All kinds of negative things were going through my mind.

Maybe He didn't care as much for Lazarus as we thought He did!

Maybe Mary and Martha thought more of the friendship than He did!

Were they wrong about how much they thought Jesus loved and cared for them?

Martha and Mary B clung to each other as we prepared Lazarus' body for burial.

Mary B, being the more vocal of the two, began murmuring to herself.

"Well ... if I'd known this was how it was going to end ... I would have saved that special perfume that I poured on His feet a few weeks ago. I would have saved it to anoint my brother's dead body for burial ..."

"What?" I asked her. "What are you talking about?"

"Oh, a few weeks ago Jesus came to see us, and I had a bottle of perfume I had been saving for possibly when I got married. But something inside of me told me to anoint Jesus' feet with it. So, I did."

"Now I'm not so sure I did the right thing ..." she added, her voice trailing off.

Disappointment.

Disillusionment.

I could see it on their faces. Were they wrong to trust

Jesus?

Then I thought ... *"Surely He'll at least show up for the funeral."*

But, no ...

As the last words were spoken over Lazarus, all I could think was ... *"This should be Jesus speaking the final words over His friend ..."*

Then we started hearing the stories of how Jesus, while He was in Nain, raised a widow woman's son from the dead.

We also heard that he had raised from the dead the daughter of Jairus.

However, in each of these incidents He raised them from the dead shortly after each one had died.

One day after the funeral, and still no Jesus.

Two days after the funeral, and still no Jesus.

Three days after the funeral, and still no Jesus.

I mean, how hard would it have been for Him to at least send us a message and let us know *why* He hadn't showed up?

I decided that Maggie and I would stay and see if we could be of some comfort.

We cleaned their house, fixed meals, and cried and prayed with Martha and Mary.

Four days later, Maggie and I were packing up and getting ready to go back home when one of Lazarus' friends came running into the house shouting, "Guess who was just spotted outside of town? *Jesus!*"

I could tell from how red Martha's face was, that she was LIVID!

She slammed down the towel she had in hand, took off her apron, wadded it up and tossed it onto the kitchen table; and out the back door she went as fast as she could go!

"Where are you going?" I shouted out the back door after her.

Turning, with her hands emphatically on her hips, she responded, *"Where do you think I'm going?"*

Before I could answer, she added, *"I'm going to find out what was more important than our dead brother!"*

I decided to follow her, just in case her mouth got her in trouble.

Turning to Maggie, I told her, "Go find Mary B and let her know that Jesus is here."

Then I turned and ran after Martha as quickly as I could.

When I got to the crowd that was gathered around Jesus, Martha was already talking to Jesus.

She was right up in His face.

"Lord, if You had been here, my brother would not have died," she was saying, with tears streaming down her face and her voice shaking with emotion.

I moved in closer to hear what excuse Jesus would give her. But He said nothing.

He simply looked at her. I could see that Jesus was deeply moved by her grief.

Then something changed in Martha. I don't know if it was the look in Jesus' eyes, or if it was the way He reached out and took her in His arms. But I could hear a glimmer of hope in her voice as she whimpered, *"... but even now I know that whatever You ask of God, God will give You ..."*

Then Jesus took her tear-stained face in His hands and said to her, "Your brother will rise again."

I was thinking the same thing that Martha was when she responded, "I know that he will rise again in the resurrection at the last day."

But Jesus turned her face upwards, looked her in the eyes and said emphatically to her, *"I am the resurrection and the life. He who believes in Me, though he may die, he shall live. And whoever lives and believes in Me shall never die.* **Do you believe this?"**

Then I felt it.

Jesus was up to something! He wasn't late at all!!!

Martha wiped her eyes, stood a little taller, and said to Him, *"Yes, Lord, I believe that You are the Christ, the Son of God, who is to come into the world."*

Then Jesus asked, "Where is Mary? I need to talk to Mary."

"Stay right here," Martha answered. "I'll go get her."

"I think she is still at your house," I shouted to Martha as she turned and ran in search of her sister.

As we stood there waiting for them to return, I thought to myself, *"If Jesus thought Martha was upset, just wait 'til*

Mary B gets here. This is NOT going to be pretty!"

However, as soon as Mary approached Jesus, she fell down at His feet and said the exact same thing Martha said. *"Lord, if You had been here, my brother would not have died."*

I had seen Jesus moved emotionally on numerous occasions, but I had never seen Him moved to this degree. When Jesus saw the way Mary B was weeping, He groaned in His spirit and was clearly troubled.

Taking Mary B by the hand, He lifted her up and asked, "Where have you laid him?"

One of those standing by said to Him, "Lord, come and see."

Then, without embarrassment or shame, Jesus wept.

All doubt about whether Jesus really cared about Lazarus was gone, as we saw His shoulders shaking and the tears streaming down His face.

"See how He loved him!" I heard someone say.

By now quite a crowd had gathered and were following as we made our way to where Lazarus was buried.

I watched intently as Jesus groaned again as He came close to the tomb.

I could see that it was a like a cave, and someone had laid a stone against the entrance.

"Take away the stone," Jesus said, wiping the tears from His eyes and clearing His voice.

I'm sure all of us were thinking it, but Martha was the one

that blurted it out.

"Lord, are You sure about this? He's been dead for four days. By now his body has started to decay and will smell something awful!"

"I know," Jesus answered. "But did I not say to you that if you would believe you would see the glory of God?"

Turning back to the tomb, He pointed to two of the bigger men there, "You two ... take the stone away!"

Martha was right. As soon as the stone that sealed the tomb was moved, we were greeted by the nauseating smell of decaying flesh.

Everyone covered their mouths and noses with their hands, and took a few steps backwards, gasping for air.

Everyone, that is, except Jesus.

It didn't seem to faze Jesus one bit.

Jesus lifted up His eyes and said, *"Father, I thank You that You have heard Me. And I know that You always hear Me, but because of the people who are standing by I said this, that they may believe that You sent Me."*

Then Jesus cleared His voice once more ... raised His hands toward heaven, and shouted with a loud authoritative voice, **"Lazarus ... come forth!"**

I don't mind telling you that the eyes of every person there that day was completely focused on the entrance of that tomb.

Was Lazarus really going to "come forth?"

I know it was only a matter of a few seconds, but it seemed

like several minutes ... Then, just as Jesus commanded him, here came Lazarus, hopping out of the grave with his hands and his feet bound together, all wrapped up in graveclothes, and his face still wrapped with a cloth.

Now that I think about it, it was rather comical.

However, we were all so entranced by what we were witnessing everyone was frozen in amazement, until Jesus, with a slight grin on His face, spoke up and said, "Will someone loose him and let him go?"

I watched the mixed reaction of the crowd. Some were so scared they turned and took off running as fast as their legs could carry them. Others fell to their knees, realizing they had just witnessed a miraculous resurrection.

But my main focus was on Martha, and Mary B. as they ran quickly to where Lazarus was standing and began unwrapping him like he was a huge present!

As soon as they unwrapped his face, he looked at them, slightly confused. Then he looked around and saw the tomb. Then he looked at the grave clothes laying at his feet. Then it HIT HIM!

"Was I DEAD?" he asked.

"Yes!" Martha shouted. "But you're not dead anymore!"

They were linked together in a circle with their hands over each other's shoulders, laughing and dancing as they twirled around in a circle!

I thought to myself ... *those silly Sadducees don't know what they are talking about. No resurrection? I wish they were here to witness THIS!*
Note: All references and quotes in this chapter were taken from the eleventh chapter of John.

CHAPTER THIRTY-TWO

Needless to say, the village of Bethany was changed that day.

Mary B told us that long after Jesus and the disciples had moved on, people were still stopping by their house to talk to Lazarus and hear his story.

Some had attended Lazarus' funeral, and they wanted to see for themselves that he was actually resurrected.

Others wanted to know more about Jesus.

She said that just about everyone they talked to about Lazarus' resurrection, ended up putting their faith in Jesus.

The second part of the miracle that happened that day was that Lazarus was also healed of whatever it was that caused his death! There were no side effects from him being dead for four days!

However, as difficult as it may be to believe, Mary B said there were a few people from Bethany that still did not trust Jesus, so they went to the Pharisee leaders and tried to stir up problems for Jesus.

Instead of being happy that Jesus had raised Lazarus from the dead, we found out that some of the religious leaders were more concerned that if Jesus kept on performing miracles, *"Everyone will believe in Him, and the Romans will come and take away both our place and nation."*

One of my friends told me he overheard Caiaphas, the high priest, actually say, *"You know nothing at all, nor do you consider that it is expedient for us that one man should die*

for the people, and not that the whole nation should perish."
Maggie and I couldn't believe it.

"You mean Caiaphas was suggesting it would be better for the Pharisees, if Jesus were to die?" Maggie asked.

As difficult as it was for us to believe and understand, the religious leaders were actually beginning to try to figure out a way to kill Jesus!

Maggie asked me, "Do you think that when Jesus told the story about the man that was beaten and robbed, and the Priest and the Levite did nothing to help him, while the good Samaritan went out of his way to help him ... do you think that is why they hate Jesus so much!?"

"Oh, my goodness!" I exclaimed. "I bet you are right! I'm sure they didn't like it when Jesus called them out for being the hypocrites that they are!"

We noticed after that time; Jesus was much more careful about making public appearances.

A few weeks later, after things went back to normal, Lazarus, Martha and Mary B stopped by to see us.

As we relived the memories of that day when Jesus raised Lazarus from the dead, Martha began telling us what she had said to Jesus, "When I met Jesus, I just bluntly told Him, 'If You had been here ... my brother would not have died!'"

"Oh, my goodness! I told Him the exact same thing," Mary B interrupted.

"How did He respond?" I asked Martha.

"He didn't say anything. He just looked at me. But I could tell by the compassion in His eyes that He was hurt deeply by Lazarus' death."

"So, I just told Him, 'Listen, I know even now God will give You whatever You ask.'"

"What did He say to that?" I asked.

"Well … He told me our brother would rise again."

"Did you understand He was talking about raising Lazarus from the dead?" I asked.

"No. Not at all. I thought He was talking about the resurrection at the last day. Then He said something that has really stuck with me. He said, 'I am the resurrection and the life. He who believes in Me, though he may die, he shall live. Whoever lives and believes in Me shall never die.'"

"What did that mean, *'Whosoever believes in Him shall never die?'*" Maggie asked.

"Well, clearly He wasn't talking about our physical body dying. Otherwise, Lazarus would not have died. So I realized, He must have been talking about a spiritual death."

"Then He asked me a very challenging question," Martha added.

"What was that?" Maggie responded.

"He asked me, 'Do you believe this?'"

"So, what did you say in response?" Maggie replied.

"I'll never forget how I answered Him. I told Him, "Yes, Lord, I believe that You are the Christ, the Son of God, who is to come into the world."

Lazarus, Martha, Mary B and Maggie knew Jesus was special. They knew He was a great teacher. They knew He had the power to perform miracles. Now they knew HE WAS THE MESSIAH!

They knew, without a doubt, just like I did, that He WAS THE CHRIST!

They knew without a doubt, just like I did, that He WAS THE SON OF GOD!

Note: All references and quotes were taken from the eleventh chapter of John.

MARY, MOTHER OF JAMES & JOSES

Matthew 27:56
among whom were Mary Magdalene, Mary the mother of James and Joses (Joseph), and the mother of Zebedee's sons.

Mark 15:40 There were also women looking on from afar, among whom were Mary Magdalene, Mary the mother of James the Less ...

Matthew 10:3
Philip and Bartholomew; Thomas and Matthew the tax collector; James the son of Alphaeus (Clophas) ...

Authors Note:
Scholars believe that Joseph, the foster father of Jesus, had a sister named Mary. This Mary was the mother of James the Less and Joses. Her husband was named Alphaeus (Clophas), making James and Joses (Joseph) cousins of Jesus Christ, on Joseph's side of the family. Joses was also called Joseph or Judas.

CHAPTER THIRTY-THREE

Cousins.

Well, they were cousins in name. They were not blood cousins.

Jesus chose two of His cousins, on Joseph's side of the family, to be His disciples.

Joseph, the earthly father of Jesus, came from a large family and one of his sisters was named Mary. Mary married a man by the name of Alphaeus, and they had twin sons named James and Joses, who became followers of Jesus Christ.

Thus, with Mary and Alphaeus being the aunt and uncle of Jesus, that made James and Joses cousins of Jesus

As a child and teenager, Jesus grew up around James and Joses in Nazareth. They spent time together at family get-togethers.

James and Joses were fine young men, never creating any problems for Mary and Alphaeus. They attended classes at the Synagogue faithfully, and were diligent in learning the scriptures.

However, as they grew into the teen years and then young adulthood, they had a difficult time finding their place in life. Every so often they came up with some wild idea that always ended in failure.

Both found wonderful mates, got married and had children, but they drifted from job to job.

Mary was so happy when both of them got married.

She was even happier when they made her a grandmother ... several times over.

James married a wonderful young lady named Dorcus, and had three children. Joses married a wonderful young lady name Anne, and they had two children.

Then Jesus called them to be His disciples.

CHAPTER THIRTY-FOUR

I was quite surprised when Mary and Alphaeus showed up on my doorstep a few weeks before Jesus performed the miracle of turning water into wine.

Mary had tears streaming down her face and Alphaeus was clearly stressed.

"What's wrong?" I asked her.

"James and Joses are leaving their wives and children!" she answered, throwing herself into my arms.

At first, I thought she meant they were leaving their wives for other women.

"Oh, no, it's not that ..." Mary said quickly, realizing I had misunderstood what she meant. "They said they are leaving to follow after Jesus."

"*Jesus*?" I asked. "My *Jesus*?"

"Yes. Your Jesus! But honestly, I've never seen them this excited before."

"So, why are you so upset?" I asked.

"How are Dorcus and Anne supposed to take care of their kids without James and Joses there to provide?" she demanded. "What are they supposed to do?"

I knew Jesus was calling men to become His disciples, but I guess it had never occurred to me that some of those men had wives and families they were leaving behind to follow Jesus.

I was definitely surprised to hear that Jesus had asked James and Joses to follow after Him. In my opinion they had very few leadership abilities.

"Oh my. Come on in and let's talk about this," I said to them both. "Let me get you a glass of water, and let's sit down and talk."

I took my time getting each of them something to drink, giving them a few minutes to settle down.

After taking a long drink, Mary asked me point blank. "So, what is Jesus up to? Why is He gathering these young men to follow after Him? He's not wanting to overthrow the Roman government in Jerusalem, is He?"

"No …" I reassured her, "Jesus is not out to try to overthrow the government."

"Then why is He gathering so many young men to follow after Him?"

I wasn't quite sure how to respond, without going into deeper detail.

"I know this may be hard for you guys to grasp, but I need to tell you who Jesus really is," I finally stated.

Puzzled, she wiped the tears from her eyes. "Who Jesus really is? Jesus is your son, isn't He?"

"Yes. But there is a lot more to the story."

Mary and Alphaeus exchanged looks that told me they did not know the truth about the birth of Jesus.

"Mary, I know Joseph was your brother, but how much did he share with you concerning the birth of Jesus?" I asked.

"Can I be honest with you?" she asked, scrunching her face together.

I could tell from the way she was acting that this was a sensitive subject with Joseph's side of the family.

"Of course, you can be honest with me," I responded.

She scratched the top of her head, as she pondered what to say next.

"WE KNOW!" she blurted out.

"You know what?" I replied, with some hesitation.

"We know that you were pregnant before you and Joseph got married!"

I couldn't help but smile as I replied, "But do you know the *whole* story?"

"Well," she hesitated, "we know what Joseph *told* us."

"Which was …"

Once more she scrunched her face up, trying to figure out how to say what she wanted to say.

"Something crazy!" she blurted out.

Then taking a big breath she continued. "He said that you were still a virgin when you got pregnant, and an angel showed up and told the both of you that you were going to have a baby, and that baby was going to be the Messiah …"

I couldn't help but laugh out loud.

Barely taking a breath she continued. "Our whole side of the family has thought you both were delusional. Either that, or you were making it up to cover up the fact that you two had relations before you got married!"

I could tell she was suddenly afraid she had gone too far as she quickly put her hand over her own mouth in an attempt to take back what she had said so candidly.

"It's okay, Mary," I said, laughing out loud again. "I completely understand. I'm sure I'd feel the same way if someone said that to me. It IS a crazy story. But it is TRUE!"

I could tell they were not convinced.

"Okay guys, hang on to your chair, because I have quite the story to tell you."

I started at the beginning, telling them about the angels, the conception, the shepherds and the wisemen.

Needless to say, there were times both of their mouths dropped open in disbelief.

When I finished, I just sat there looking at them, and they just sat there looking back at me.

"Really?" Mary finally asked.

"Yes. Really!"

"You're not kidding me?"

"Nope. I'm not kidding you."

Finally, Alphaeus spoke up. "So, you're telling us that Jesus is truly the Messiah? The Son of God?"

"That's exactly what I'm telling you!"

I could see they were both trying to process what I had shared with them.

"So ... what is Jesus doing?" Alphaeus asked. "What is His plan? If He's not planning on getting rid of the Roman oppression we're under, what is His purpose?"

"Those are all great questions," I responded. "But to be honest with you, I don't know for sure what His plan is ... other than to do what God tells Him to do."

Finally, Mary asked, "So, is it okay if I share this with Dorcus and Anne? They are worried sick that James and Judas are off on some wild goose chase again."

I couldn't help but laugh out loud once more.

Grinning herself, Mary added, "I'm serious. Those two boys have really struggled finding their place in this world."

"That's putting it mildly," Alphaeus added. "Maybe spending some time with Jesus will be good for them."

"Yes, it's okay to share this with Dorcus and Anne," I replied. "But don't be surprised if they find it hard to believe. That's why I don't share this with a lot of people!"

They both stood, gave me the biggest hug, and thanked me.

On the way out the door Mary turned and laughingly said, "So, in a way, our whole family is related to the Messiah!"

"That you are!"

CHAPTER THIRTY-FIVE

A few days later Mary returned to my house to update me on how things went when she shared the truth about Jesus with Dorcas and Anne.

"So, you told them Jesus is the Messiah?" I asked.

"Well, not right away. I wanted to hear what they had to say first."

She said as soon as she got home, she and Alphaeus called the whole family together to talk about James' and Joses' decision to leave and follow Jesus.

"It turned out to be a wonderful conversation," Mary stated.

"So, you told them about Jesus being the Messiah?" I repeated.

"Yes. But Mary, it's still a whole lot for any of us to take in."

"Oh, I get that," I told her.

"They reassured us that they were not abandoning their families, but this was something they *'just had to do'* was how they put it.

"James said, even though Jesus is their cousin, there's something special about the way He speaks. They went on and on about the authority that's in His voice when He speaks."

"Have either of you attended any of Jesus' meetings?" I asked.

"No," Mary replied. "But it sounds like it's something we should put on our to-do list."

"Promise me that you will take time to go hear Him speak. And take Dorcus and Anne with you. I'm sure any doubts you have about His purpose will be answered."

"We promise!"

CHAPTER THIRTY-SIX

When Mary and Alphaeus returned home, James and Joses met them at the door.

James spoke first.

"Would you guys like to talk to Jesus?" James asked his mother and father.

"Your mother and I were just talking about that very thing," Alphaeus replied. "Maybe we could go hear Jesus speak sometime."

"What about us bringing Jesus here to talk to you?" Joses said. "Would that be okay?"

"Oh, that would be more than okay. That would be wonderful!" Mary responded.

They were so excited they nearly knocked each other down, rushing out the door.

"We'll be right back," James shouted over his shoulder as they both ran off like two boys off on a wild adventure.

Mary and Alphaeus smiled at each other.

It was hard to not get caught up in their excitement.

Twenty minutes later she heard the sound of laughter, and stepped outside.

Mary laughed out loud when she saw them returning. Her two sons were on each side of Jesus, dragging Him so quickly they were almost pulling Him off balance.

It was quite humorous seeing grown men acting like little boys.

"Okay guys, slow down. It's not a race," Jesus was saying, with a big grin on His face.

Arriving, they were breathless with excitement, and were talking over the top of each other.

"Mom, this is our cousin, Jesus!"
"This is the Man we have been talking about!"
"Jesus, this is our mom."
"She is the best mom in the world!"

Jesus broke free from their grasp and stepped forward.

Smiling, He reached out to take both of Mary's hands in His.

"Hi Aunt Mary. Do you remember who I am?" Jesus asked.

"Of course," Mary replied, pulling Him into her arms.

"I know who You are. You're the Son of Mary and ..."

Suddenly she was speechless.

Based on what she now knew, she didn't know how to respond concerning who Jesus' Father was.

"You're the Son of Mary and ... *JOSEPH?*" she replied.

Instead of coming out as an answer, it came out as a question.

Mary's face immediately turned beet red, and Alphaeus just stood there speechless ... no help whatsoever.

Then Jesus did the unexpected.

He winked!

"It sounds like you have been talking to My mother," He responded, with a twinkle in His eyes.

Immediately Mary and Alphaeus were at ease.

"Yes," Mary replied. "She told us all about Your birth."

With a twinkle still in His eyes, Jesus responded, "so what do you think?"

Mary turned and looked at Alphaeus, then they both turned and looked at Jesus. Clearly, any doubt they may have had about Jesus evaporated into thin air.

"Honestly, I only have one question," Mary replied.

"And what question was that?"

"Will You take good care of our boys?"

CHAPTER THIRTY-SEVEN

Every few days it seemed like someone was stopping by my house to tell Maggie and I stories about the wonderful things Jesus and His disciples were doing.

One day all of Jesus' younger brothers, James, Joseph, Judas, and Simon stopped by my house.

"Would you guys like to go see what Jesus is up to these days?" I asked.

As in the past they seemed reluctant.

To entice them I added, "We can go by and see if your Aunt Mary and Uncle Alphaeus would like to go as well."

They were still hesitant.

"I'm sure your cousins, James and Joses, will be there too," I added, trying my best to entice them to go.

Maggie couldn't contain herself. She literally started jumping up and down ...

"Come on you guys! Let's go! Let's go right now!"

I could tell they weren't all that thrilled about the idea, but Maggie's exuberance won them over, and they gave in and agreed to go.

Maggie was so excited!

We packed up enough things to last a few days and set off to see if Mary and Alphaeus were able to go with us.

"Absolutely!" Mary and Alphaeus responded when we

asked them. "I've been hearing all kinds of stories," Mary added. "It sounds like Jesus and His disciples are creating quite a stir everywhere they go."

They rushed to gather some things into a satchel, and we set off as quickly as we could go.

"Do you have any idea where He is?" Mary asked.

"I have a general idea," I replied. "I heard He is traveling from village to village on the eastern side of the Sea of Galilee. Once we get close, I'm sure we'll hear from the villagers which direction He is heading."

It took us a day and a half to get there. We enjoyed our time together, but I could see that Mary was very anxious to get there as soon as possible.

"Are you more excited to see your two sons, or to see Jesus?" I jokingly asked her.

"I am excited to see James and Joses, but to be honest with you, I am more excited to see Jesus in action!"

"*In action ...*' that's a great way to describe Jesus," Maggie stated, with a smile. "If it's anything like the last time we went to see Him, there will be all kinds of action!"

Just as we thought, it was easy to find Jesus. Every village He had walked through was buzzing with excitement. The stories about the miracles He was performing were still in the air.

Following the directions of those we encountered, we found Him rather quickly. Another great crowd had gathered around Him, and He was sitting down on the hillside.

As we had done on previous visits, we tried to stay far

enough away as to not be a distraction; yet be close enough to hear and see what was going on.

Then Jesus began to speak.

I loved hearing Him speak, but I loved seeing the response from those that were listening even more.

Mary, Alphaeus, and Maggie were spell bound, as were the rest of the crowd. Even though there were several hundred people there, it was so quiet that every word that Jesus spoke could be clearly heard.

I could tell that Jesus' brothers were trying to act like they were not really that interested in what He was saying, but the longer Jesus spoke, the more they were drawn to His message.

After Jesus had been teaching for a while, someone from the crowd called out to Him that His mother and brothers were there looking for Him. (Matthew 12:47)

"Who is My mother and who are My brothers?" He asked. (Matthew 12:48)

I almost raised my hand and shouted out, "I AM!"

But something stopped me. I could tell that Jesus was trying to make a point.

Then He stretched out His hand toward His disciples, and His closest followers, and said, "Here are My mother and My brothers! For whoever does the will of My Father in heaven is My brother and sister and mother." (Matthew 12:49-50)

I looked at James, Joseph, Judas, and Simon, not sure what to expect. Would His words offend them?

In the past, when Jesus would talk about His "Heavenly Father," rather than start a debate with Jesus, they would simply get up and walk away.

However, today I saw a different response.

Maybe it was the atmosphere. Maybe it was the excitement of the crowd. Or maybe ... just maybe ... His Heavenly Father was working on their hearts and minds!

The important thing was ... they stayed.

At this point the crowd had grown so much, and was pressing forward so much, Jesus finally climbed into a boat, paddled out a short distance, and sat down and began teaching again.

Even the little children were quiet.

Every single person there seemed mesmerized by the simple stories that He told, including Mary, Alphaeus, Maggie ... *and His brothers*!

I loved how He took every day things, and used them to make a point.

He was doing that very thing again. He was talking about a farmer that went out to sow some seed, and how the seed fell on different types of ground. He talked about how the seed that fell among thorns was choked out, and the seed that fell on stony ground withered up and blew away. However, he then spoke about the seed that fell on good ground took root and began to grow.

"The seed that the farmer sowed is like the word of God," Jesus said. "When the word of God is sown, Satan comes and takes away the word that is being sown." (Matthew 13)

I loved it. It was simple, yet profound.

Again, I turned to see how His brothers were responding. Then I saw it. His brothers were suddenly beginning to see Jesus as more than just their oldest brother!

They were really listening. They were recognizing what I had always seen in Jesus.

As soon as He finished speaking, we waited patiently as He came ashore and began to minister to those that were sick and in need.

For the first time, His brothers were witnessing Jesus as a healer!

Once more, I saw a change in their attitude toward Jesus.

Finally, the crowd dispersed.

As soon as Jesus saw us, He came running as quickly as He could.

"Mom! It's so good to see you."

When He saw the rest of His brothers, Maggie, and His Aunt Mary and Uncle Alphaeus, His face exploded with a huge smile.

"Oh my," He shouted. "The whole gang is here!"

He hugged each one of us, pausing to tell Mary and Alphaeus that James and Joses were nearby.

I loved how He also took time to ask each of His brothers how they and their families were doing.

"Where are You headed next?" I asked, after He had a chance to spend some time with each one.

"Well, what do you think about Me coming back home to Nazareth with you guys?"

Needless to say, everyone was very excited.

"Is it okay if the disciples tag along?" He asked.

I thought Maggie was going to explode. "Please say yes, please say yes!"

"Yes," I replied, to Maggie's great delight.

We had the most pleasant trip back to Nazareth.

I was so excited for everyone to see Jesus.

This would be His first trip home since He began His ministry.

CHAPTER THIRTY-EIGHT

We had a wonderful time walking back home with Jesus.

He told us about more of the many miracles that had taken place recently.

"Wait a second," Simon asked, when Jesus talked about the miracle that took place on the Sea of Galilee. "The wind and waves obeyed Your command?"

I could tell Simon, and the rest of his brothers were still a little bit skeptical.

Jesus simply smiled and said, "They sure did. If you don't believe me, ask James and Joses, your cousins, the next time you see them. They were there!"

He talked about the man that was paralyzed, and the blind men that were healed.

Finally, it grew quiet.

Then, Maggie began telling her story.

Once more, I could see the hearts of Jesus' brothers changing.

When we arrived back home in Nazareth the first thing Jesus wanted to do was go to the local synagogue, one of His favorite places to go when He was younger.

Everyone else went on home, but Maggie and I followed along with Him to the synagogue.

It was hard to keep my pride under control as Jesus stepped up and began to teach.

At first, everyone seemed astonished at His words.

I could hear them whispering among themselves ... *"Where did this Man get this kind of wisdom and mighty works?"* (Mark 6:2)

Then I heard a shift in their tone ...

"But, isn't this the carpenter's son?"

"Isn't this Mary's son?"

"Isn't He just the older brother to James, Joseph, Simon, and Judas?"

"If so, where did He get all of these abilities?"

"He's no better than we are!"

I couldn't believe what I was hearing!

Couldn't they see? Couldn't they hear?

Here the Messiah was ... standing right in front of them!

Then I saw the sadness in Jesus' eyes.

Oh, how He wanted to heal them. Oh, how He wanted to perform many miracles for the lame, the blind, and deaf people that He grew up with!

Sadly, I watched as He turned and began to walk away, murmuring, *"a prophet is not without honor except in his own country and in his own house."* (Matthew 13:57)

That was the last time Jesus visited His home town.

All I could think was ... *what could have been!*

CHAPTER THIRTY-NINE

Every time Mary and Alphaeus let us know that James and Joses were back home, Maggie and I would rush over to their house to see them, and to find out the latest exciting adventure they had been on with Jesus.

They told stories about blind people being healed, deaf ears being unstopped, and crippled limbs being made straight.

We listened for hours, as they told story after story.

"He even touched and healed several lepers!" James said.

"He *touched* them?" Maggie asked, knowing that touching a leper was not socially acceptable.

"Oh, yes," Joses replied. "It's like there is nothing too big or impossible for Him."

Turning to me Joses asked, "Do you know where the town of Nain is?"

I shook my head up and down.

"We were entering Nain," Joses continued, "and there coming down the street was a funeral procession. Jesus turned to us and told us to stop walking. He said there was something He needed to take care of. We watched intently, as Jesus walked over to one of the mourners and asked who it was that had died. They said that it was a young man."

James took over the story. "We could tell that Jesus was really touched by the young man's mother, who was just sobbing and sobbing uncontrollably."

Every eye was now on James, as the excitement rose in his voice.

"Then Jesus casually walked over to the coffin, reached out and touched it, and said, *'Young man I say to you, arise!'*"

James paused, amused at how intensely we all were listening.

"So...WHAT HAPPENED?" Maggie shouted, aggravated that they stopped the story.

James leaned in close to all of us, and said ... "The young man ... SAT UP!"

I about fell off my chair!

"He SAT UP???" Maggie shouted.

"Yes. He just ... SAT UP ... right there in the coffin and started talking!"

"And you two were right there and saw it with your own eyes?" Maggie asked.

Both of them shook their heads up and down. "We sure did," they responded in unison.

I couldn't help myself. I just had to know.

"So, what did he say? What did the young man say?"

"He said, *'Where is my mom?'*"

"Aw ..." Maggie said. "He wanted his mommy!"

"What did Jesus do?" I asked.

"Jesus turned, grabbed his mother, and said, *'here she is!'*"

It took several seconds for us to wrap our minds around the story we had just heard.

Then Maggie, just being Maggie, started in with the questions …

"How did he get out of the coffin?"…
"Did he remember being dead?"…
"What did his mother say?"…
"What did they do with the used coffin?"

We all burst into laughter.

I could see that Mary still had some questions, so I interrupted.

"James, Joses, this is all wonderful, but I think your mother has a more serious question."

"Yes, I sure do," she responded.

Turning to her two sons, she said, "Okay, tell me what a normal day is like with Jesus."

For the next hour they took turns, each one telling how much they loved being with Jesus. They talked about more of His miracles, and about some of the parables He told.

They shared how they didn't always understand some of the philosophical discussions or theological debates Jesus had with Luke and John, but they said they were just happy to be there.

"So, do you each have jobs that you're supposed to do?" Alphaeus asked.

"Oh yes," James stated.

They shared how they had the responsibility of watching over the multitudes when a crowd would gather around Jesus.

"We're ushers," Joses stated. "We keep an eye on the crowds to make sure everyone stays under control ... especially when Jesus starts healing people. People can get rather rowdy. Everyone wants to get to the front of the line, and sometimes they can get rather pushy."

"Yes, Jesus likes things done decently and in order," James added. "When a large crowd starts gathering, He likes for us to seat people in groups of fifty or a hundred each."

"We're kind of the 'gofers' of the group," James added. "We help Phillip with the supplies, and we help Nathaniel deliver money to families that are in need. We just like helping anyone and everyone, whenever they need a helping hand."

Mary and Alphaeus were so very proud of their sons.

They could see that the boys had found their place. Was it among the elite of the disciples? No. But James and Joses were fine with that, and so were they.

I could see they didn't mind at all being called *the least of the apostles*. They were happy just to be a part of something so exciting and meaningful.

It was wonderful seeing the joy on Mary and Alphaeus' faces.

Their sons had finally found their place in this world.

THE OTHER MARY

Matthew 27:61
And Mary Magdalene was there, and the other Mary, sitting opposite the tomb.

Matthew 28:1
Now after the Sabbath, as the first day of the week began to dawn, Mary Magdalene and the other Mary came to see the tomb.

CHAPTER FORTY

Invisible.

That was how she felt.

Invisible.

Quiet ... shy ... backwards ... timid ..., an accurate description of the *other* Mary, as she was known.

A widow at the age of forty.

She and her husband Zachariah never had any children.

So, when he suddenly passed way, Mary was left feeling quite alone.

Invisible.

There were no close relatives.

Both of Mary's parents had also passed away when she was young, so she spent most of her time, hiding away from the world.

That is, until she became a neighbor of Mary, the mother of Jesus, and her husband Joseph.

When Zachariah passed away, Mary and Joseph took her under their wings and began helping her with chores around the house. From time to time, they would help her out with leftover food, and clothing from the used clothing market.

In return, she would help Mary and Joseph out by taking care of Jesus from time to time when He was small.

Then, as the other children came along, she would babysit for them as well.

However, outside of her relationship with Mary, Joseph, and their family, she still felt ... invisible.

Mary quickly developed quite a fondness for Jesus. He was like she was in many ways. Rather quiet, shy and backwards. He was a very easy child to take care of ... and love.

Their relationship grew to the point that the other Mary was one of the few people that Mary shared the more intimate details with, concerning the conception and birth of Jesus.

The other Mary knew intimately the story about Jesus getting left behind in Jerusalem when He was twelve years old.

She saw the challenges that Jesus faced as He grew into His teenage years.

She could see that He felt different than the other children.

As the other siblings were born, she could also see that more and more responsibility was thrust on His young shoulders.

She admired how He was such a good big brother. How He always watched out for His younger siblings.

She watched as He grew into a teenager, and then into a young man.

Years later when Joseph passed away, Mary and the other Mary's friendship grew closer as they each had suffered similar tragic losses.

Then as Jesus began working, she admired His carpentry skills.

She wondered if He would ever find the "right" woman and settle into a life with a wife and children of His own. However, she struggled with how that could work out with His being the Messiah.

So no, she was never in the limelight when it came to Jesus and His ministry.

She didn't have an amazing testimony like Mary Magdalene. She had never been demon possessed. In fact, she didn't even know what it was like to be healed by Jesus.

Jesus was very young and had not started His ministry yet when Zachariah, her husband, died. So, there wasn't even the opportunity for Jesus to raise him from the dead the way He did for Mary, the sister of Lazarus.

She didn't have any children, so there was no opportunity for one of her sons to become a disciple of Jesus the way Mary and Alphaeus's sons were.

When it came to the hierarchy of importance among the Marys in the life of Jesus, she felt like she was delegated to being the lowest one on the list.

She was simply *the other Mary.*

She always felt like her name was always the last name on the list, when it came to being invited over for get-togethers, or to weddings.

Loved? Yes.

Important? No.

CHAPTER FORTY-ONE

It sounded like someone was trying to break my front door down they were banging on it so hard.

Maggie and I both made it to the front door at the same time.

Standing at the door was Mary, the sister of Lazarus.

"He's been arrested!" she shouted, with tears streaming down her face.

"They have arrested Him!" she repeated.

I wasn't sure who she was talking about.

With John the Baptist being arrested and then beheaded, I knew that all of the disciples were in danger of being arrested at any time.

I grabbed her by the shoulders.

"Who? Who has been arrested?"

She could barely get herself to speak His name.

"Jesus ..."

I felt strength leave my entire body, and my knees buckled as I collapsed to the floor.

Oh no! This was it!

Maggie quickly gathered me in her arms and began patting my face.

Slowly I felt my wits gathering.

"Go get a wet cloth!" Maggie shouted to Mary.

"*What's happening?*" Maggie whispered loudly in my ear, holding me tight with one hand, and patting my face with the other.

"I don't know …"

"What should we do?" she asked.

I felt my strength coming back, so with Maggie's help I staggered to my feet and sat down on the couch.

"Well, we can't sit here and do *nothing*!" I said with my head in my hands.

"I know," Maggie responded. "Why don't we start by gathering up everyone we know that is one of His followers?"

"That's a great idea!"

Mary returned with the damp cloth, sat down beside me, and began wiping my face.

Turning to her I asked, "Who told you that He had been arrested?"

"Oh, it's spreading through Jerusalem like a wild fire. Someone that knew we were close friends came and told me. Then I came here as quickly as I could."

"What time is it?" I asked, still a little groggy.

"It's around three o'clock in the morning," Mary answered.

I was starting to think clearly again.

"Okay, here is what we are going to do," I stated, feeling my voice get stronger.

"Mary, where was He when He was arrested?"

"In the Garden of Gethsemane."

"Maggie, more than likely they will be taking Him to Pilate, so I want you to get there as quickly as you can."

"What do you want me to do when I get there?"

"Just try to put yourself in a position where Jesus can see you, so that He knows that we know what is going on."

"What do you want me to do?" Mary asked.

"Go get Martha and Lazarus, gather up as many followers of Jesus as you can, and tell them to gather outside of Pilate's palace."

"What are you going to do?" Maggie asked, giving me a quick hug as she left.

"I'm going to start gathering up as many supporters as I can as well. I'll meet you at Pilate's gate."

CHAPTER FORTY-TWO

The sun was just beginning to rise when I arrived at Pilate's palace with about thirty other people that I knew were believers in Jesus.

Maggie, Mary, Martha and Lazarus were already there, with another thirty or forty of Jesus' supporters they had picked up along the way as well.

As soon as I arrived, John the Beloved came running up to me and gathered me up into his big burly arms.

He was sobbing uncontrollably.

Finally, he gathered himself.

"Is Jesus inside?" I asked.

"Yes. The chief priests and some Roman soldiers have arrested Him and taken Him before Pilate."

"What is the charge against Him?" I asked.

"Blasphemy. They were saying that by Him stating He is the Son of God, He has committed blasphemy."

I shuddered. I knew enough about the law to know that if someone was found guilty of blasphemy, they could be executed at the word of the high priest.

"Oh Mary! It was awful! Just awful!" John continued. "Judas betrayed Jesus by kissing Him on the cheek!"

On one hand I was shocked that Judas Iscariot would actually betray my son, but on the other hand, there was something about Judas that I just had never trusted.

"So, what happened?"

"Jesus was praying in the garden. He asked several of us to pray with Him, but it was so late, and we were so tired, we kept falling asleep."

I could see that John felt like it was partially his fault.

"Maybe if we had been awake, we could have prevented them from getting to Him ..." he said, his voice trailing off in despair.

"No," I replied. "This was bound to happen sooner or later. I'm just glad that you were there with Him."

"Peter did what he could. He pulled his sword to defend Jesus, and took a swipe at one of the men there to arrest him, but thankfully he only cut off the man's ear."

Despite the dire circumstances, I found myself smiling slightly.

"Now that doesn't surprise me one bit. Peter has always had a little bit of an attitude," I responded.

"That's putting it mildly," John replied. "But you'll never guess how Jesus responded."

"My guess is that He scolded Peter," I responded.

"Exactly! He scolded him. But then He reached down and picked up the man's ear, placed it back on his head, and his ear was instantly reattached!"

After all of the miracles Jesus performed, I don't know why this one caught me so off guard.

"What? He healed one of the men that was there to arrest

Him?" I asked, shaking my head in wonder.

Maggie and some of the other women walked up in time to hear what Jesus did with the man's ear.

Maggie, of course, had to speak up.

"So, did the man that got healed stand up against the rest of those that were there to arrest Jesus?" she asked gruffly, placing her hands on her hips defiantly.

"No," John responded. Then hanging his head, he added, "Unfortunately, when it became apparent that Jesus was indeed going to be taken away, the whole bunch of us fled in fear of being arrested as well."

With that admission, tears began running down John's rugged face again.

"So, is that why you're the only one here?" I asked. "The rest of them ran away?"

"I am ashamed to admit it, but it's true. All of us failed Jesus."

I could see that John was really beating himself up over what had happened, so I took the conversation in a different direction.

Pointing to Pilate's palace I asked, "So, is Jesus inside?"

Before John could answer we saw the front gate to the palace open, and a throng of soldiers, along with several of the high priests, came hustling through the gate, and there in the center of the throng was Jesus.

By now some of the priests had gathered up some of their own followers, and were starting to surround us.

I turned to the group of Jesus' followers and shouted out, "Listen up everyone. They're going to be looking for reasons to arrest anyone that opposes them."

I made it a point to make eye contact with Maggie.

"What?" she stated.

"Control yourself Maggie. Don't make things worse!"

As they marched Jesus out of the Palace gate, the soldiers kept us from getting close, but I did get close enough to see the blood pouring from Jesus' nose, and that His lips were also swollen and bleeding.

"What have you done?" I began screaming, ignoring my own advice, trying to make my way to Jesus. "What have you done to my Jesus?"

One of the soldiers shoved me so hard I fell backwards. Thankfully, John was there to catch me.

Quickly we realized that there was nothing we could do.

Then, through the throng of people, Jesus looked at me, and shook His head from side to side, telling me to stop trying to interfere.

"Where are you taking Him?" Maggie screamed at one of the priests.

"Pilate wants nothing to do with Him, so we are taking Him to King Herod," he responded, with a look of disgust on his face.

As soon as I heard the name King Herod, I felt my mind and body grow numb, and darkness overwhelmed me.

CHAPTER FORTY-THREE

When I came to myself, John was carrying me in his arms, and we were standing outside King Herod's palace. We were part of a growing crowd of followers of Jesus that were there to support Him.

"Let me down," I said to John. "I'm okay now."

"Are you sure? I don't mind carrying you."

"I'm okay. Put me down. I can stand on my own."

The shock of hearing King Herod's name had gotten the best of me. This King Herod was the son of the King Herod that made the decree thirty-three years earlier, that all baby boys under two years old, in and around Bethlehem, were to be slaughtered in an attempt to kill Jesus.

"Oh, this is not going to go well," I said, worry creeping across my face.

Taking my arm to steady me, Maggie asked, "What is it that has you so worried?"

Mary, Martha, and Lazarus gathered in closer as I began telling the sad story of the massacre at Bethlehem that took place thirty-three years earlier.

"This King Herod is that King Herod's son?" Martha asked.

"Yes. I only hope and pray that he's not as evil as his father!"

Unfortunately, I was wrong. At that exact moment King Herod, along with his men of war, were mocking Jesus, and treating Him with contempt.

Then the palace door suddenly opened and the soldiers, the priests and Jesus reappeared.

Jesus was covered with one of King Herod's fancy robes.

We were all confused.

Once again Maggie stepped forward, trying to interfere with one of the soldiers.

"What are you doing with Jesus now?" she asked. "And why did you place that robe on Him?"

"King Herod wants nothing to do with Him. We are taking Him back to Pilate," the high priest responded.

"What about the robe? Why is He wearing that fancy robe?"

Sneering, the high priest responded, "He claims to be the *King of the Jews* ... so it's only fitting your *so-called-king* should wear a royal robe!"

My heart almost stopped!

The KING OF THE JEWS ...

Those words were the words that the Wise Men used when addressing King Herod at the birth of Jesus.

Those words were the words that resulted in the baby massacre!

I couldn't help myself. I ran to Jesus!!!

"*Let Him go! Let Him go!*" I screamed, trying to fight my way to Him.

Fortunately, Lazarus caught up with me and swept me off my feet.

I collapsed into his arms.

"They're going to kill Him ..." I cried out, trying to break free from Lazarus' grasp. **"They're going to kill Him ..."**

CHAPTER FORTY-FOUR

Lazarus was still carrying me in his arms.

I just knew that King Herod was going to somehow finish the job his father started thirty-three years earlier.

I finally regained my strength and was able to walk on my own, as we made our way back to Pilate.

Mary and Martha were trying their best to reassure me.

"Mary," Martha was stating, "this may be a good thing. It looks like King Herod wanted nothing to do with Jesus, other than humiliate Him. Maybe Pilate will release him."

One of the priests ran on ahead, to let Pilate know that King Herod wanted nothing to do with Jesus, therefore, they were bringing Him back to Pilate. His fate was going to lay in the hands of Pilate.

When the throng arrived back at Pilate's palace, Pilate met us at the front gate. He then called together the priests, the rulers, and a bunch of the Pharisees, and he said to them, "You have brought this Man to me, as one who misleads the people. And indeed, having examined Him in your presence, I have found no fault in this Man concerning those things of which you accuse Him. And not only have I found no fault in Him, neither did Herod. That's why Herod sent Him back to me. Indeed, nothing deserving of death has been done by Him. Therefore, I have made the decision to chastise Him and release Him."

By now, the Pharisees had incensed the crowd to the point they rejected Pilate's decision and began shouting, "Away with this Man ... away with this Man ... release unto us Barabbas!"

Realizing that any followers of Jesus were in great danger, John gathered us together and moved us to the outskirts of the throng that were screaming and chanting for the death of Jesus.

I found myself looking into that throng of angry people, trying to see if I recognized any faces. I was looking for a familiar face that may have benefited from the thousands of miracles my Jesus had performed over the past three and a half years.

"Surely, some of those that were healed ... surely some of the thousands that were miraculously fed with the fishes and loaves will stand up and defend Jesus ..." I thought to myself.

But if anyone was objecting, their voices were being drowned out by the angry mob that was chanting for His death.

Pilate raised his hands until the rowdy crowd quieted down enough for him to speak.

Once more, he pleaded with them to allow him to severely beat Jesus, but then let Him go.

But the crowd continued chanting for His death.

Then, I saw Pilate motion to the soldiers to take Jesus back inside the palace gates.

"Now what are they doing?" Maggie asked, with terror in her voice.

"I don't know," John answered. "Maybe Pilate is going to release Him after all."

We waited ... and waited ...

The crowd continued calling out for His death.

"Crucify Him! Crucify Him!" the chanting continued.

About an hour went by, and then the palace gate opened once again.

I was absolutely horrified!!!

What had they done to my Jesus???

He was so horribly beaten; He was barely recognizable. Then I remembered one of the prophesies written by Isaiah, *"His visage was marred more than any man, and His form more than the sons of men."* (Isaiah 52:14)

His entire body was covered with blood. Blood was pouring down His face from the crown of thorns that had been thrust upon His brow. His eyes were nearly swollen shut from the blows to His face.

Then He turned and I saw His back. What I saw caused my legs to collapse, and I fell to the ground once again.

How could one human being inflict this much torment and pain upon another person?

The flesh on His back had been shredded so deeply that His muscles and even parts of His spine were exposed!

Still the crowd was not satisfied, and the chanting continued.

Crucify Him! ... Crucify Him! ...

Louder and louder, it got.

Crucify Him! ... Crucify Him! ...

I looked around to see if any more of Jesus' followers had joined us. However, the pro-Jesus crowd remained rather small.

John, Maggie, Mary, Martha, and Lazarus had been joined by Jesus' Aunt Mary, the mother of James and Joses, and the other Mary.

Everyone was visibly shaken. Tears were streaming down their worried faces.

All five Marys were there.

Helpless. Hopeless.

The chants of *crucify Him ... crucify Him ...* grew louder and louder.

Once more Pilate raised his hands until the crowd stopped shouting.

The only sound that could be heard from the crowd was the handful of Jesus' followers that were weeping.

With a look of aggravation on his face, Pilate turned to one of his servants, and gruffly shouted, *"Bring me a bowl of water!"*

Maggie asked, "What does he want with a bowl of water?"

No one had an answer.

So, everyone watched in silence as he slowly began to wash his hands.

When he finished washing his hands, he lifted his face to the crowd and shouted out, with anger still dripping from each word, "I am innocent of the blood of this just Man. Go ahead and do what you wish with Him!" (Matthew 27:24)

Then he quickly turned and walked back inside the palace gates.

CHAPTER FORTY-FIVE

As the chants of *Crucify Him! ... Crucify Him! ...* started up again, the crowd gathered around the Roman soldiers as a cross suddenly appeared out of nowhere.

John and Lazarus were basically carrying me, one of my arms in each of their grasps.

Then the crowd began following the soldiers and Jesus.

"Get as close as you can," I said to John. "I want Jesus to be able to see me. I want Him to know that I am with Him!"

So, we shoved and elbowed our way through the crowd until we somehow made our way to the front.

The chant continued, as the soldiers thrust the cross on Jesus' back, forcing Him to carry His own cross as we began the journey to Golgotha.

I could see His strength leaving His body as His legs began quivering beneath the heavy load. So much blood had poured down His body, it had saturated His feet, causing His feet to slip and slide on the cobblestone roadway.

Finally, He fell completely to the ground.

I watched in horror, as over and over He tried to get back up. But the weight of the cross was too much for Him to bear.

The whole time the soldiers were shouting at Him and cursing Him ... demanding that He get back up.

A few minutes earlier I noticed a man that seemed to be following along with us, and I could tell by the look on his face that he did not agree with what was going on.

Realizing Jesus had gone as far as He could go, one of the Roman soldiers came over to the man that had joined us, and shoved him toward Jesus.

"Pick up His cross!" the soldier bellowed at the man.

We later found out that his name was Simon. He was from Cyrene, and he was in Jerusalem to celebrate the Passover.

As Simon bent to pick up the cross, he turned slightly so that we made eye contact, and I mouthed the words ... *"Thank you!"*

He nodded his head slightly in acknowledgement.

I tried to make my way to Jesus' side, but the soldiers were keeping everyone away.

So, we followed.

Mary Magdalene followed. Mary, the mother of James and Joses followed. Mary, Martha, and Lazarus followed. And the other Mary followed.

Then I saw it, and I froze in place for a split second. There on the cobblestone street was a trail of Jesus' blood! And the irony struck me, this crowd that was shouting for the death of my Jesus was literally trampling His blood beneath their feet!

Slowly we made our way to Calvary.

At first, I was relieved when the chanting stopped. But then I realized we had reached the place where He was going to be crucified.

The throng was now silent. Eerily silent.

Turning to the crowd, Jesus slowly looked into the faces of everyone close enough to hear His weakened voice, and He said, "Daughters of Jerusalem, do not weep for Me, but weep for yourselves and for your children. For indeed the days are coming when you will say, 'Blessed are the barren, wombs that never bore, and breasts that never nursed!"

No one moved. No one spoke a word. Jesus turned, and looked at each one of us.

"Then they will begin to say to the mountains," He continued, "'Fall on us!' They will say to the hills, 'cover us!'" (Luke 23:28-29)

The only sound I could hear was the quiet weeping of those near us.

Simon slowly and reverently lowered the cross to the ground, and came and stood with us.

A Roman soldier took an aggressive step toward Jesus, but Jesus held up His hand and stopped him.

We all watched in complete amazement as Jesus weakly walked over to where the cross lay on the ground. Then, looking the soldier square in the face, He willingly laid Himself prostrate on the cross, stretched out His hands and closed His eyes in submission.

The stillness of the moment was deafening.

No one spoke.

No more chanting.

Then Jesus opened His eyes, turned His head, and looked

directly at me.

My Jesus ... My son ... My child.

I forced myself to maintain eye contact with Him as the shadow of the hammer being raised crossed His face.

The pain in His eyes was matched with the sound of the hammer striking the nail, as the first blow was struck.

He and I winced in unison as the repeating sound of metal on metal echoed into the silence ... as blow after blow was struck, driving the nail through His flesh and deep into the cross.

Thankfully, John and Lazarus were still supporting me, their hands beneath my arms.

I felt their bodies convulse along with mine every time another resounding blow of the hammer was struck.

But my eyes never left His eyes.

The torture continued on as the hammer was raised to secure His other arm to the cross.

Again, we all winced in unison with Jesus, as the second nail was driven into His other hand.

I wanted to help Him. I wanted to fight the soldiers. I wanted to take Him home with me, and take care of the many wounds that were inflicted on His body.

Instead, the only thing I could do was watch.

Not once did Jesus try to pull His hands away.

Then, He willingly crossed His ankles.

Once more, I saw the shadow of the hammer.

"Don't look away," I told myself. *"Jesus needs you. Don't look away!"*

Finally, the sound of the hammering stopped.

Once again, there was complete silence.

It was as if all creation had stopped what it was doing, and was standing at attention as the Creator was laying down His life.

As soon as the nail in His feet was secure, several more soldiers stepped closer to help pick up Jesus and the cross. As they prepared to raise the cross, one of them hung a sign on the top of the cross which said, JESUS OF NAZARETH, THE KING OF THE JEWS.

They roughly positioned the bottom of the cross so that it would fall into the hole in the ground and slowly the cross was raised.

Still, I refused to lose eye contact with Jesus.

When the cross fell into place with a sickening *thud,* Jesus and I once more winced in unison.

Then, one of the soldiers walked up to Jesus and began removing His garments.

Maggie took a step forward and shouted, "Stop it! Stop it! Haven't you done enough?"

The soldier simply grinned, and walked away with His garment.

It was all I could bear to do nothing, as Jesus' naked body was exposed for all to see.

My Jesus ... My son ... My child.

The soldier who took His clothes motioned for several of the other soldiers to gather around him. They knelt on the ground and began gambling to see who would get His garments.

In doing so, they fulfilled a prophecy that had been written by King David when he penned the words, *"They divided My garments among them, and for My clothing they cast lots."* (Psalm 22:18)

It was as if Jesus could sense the anger and frustration I was dealing with.

I was angry at the High Priest. I was angry at Pilate. I was angry at Caesar. I was angry with the Roman soldiers.

I was angry there weren't more of His so-called followers and disciples there to defend Him.

Yes, Jesus knew what I was dealing with. Because He did something that no one saw coming. It was as if He commanded everyone's attention without saying a word and then He began to speak.

"Father, forgive them, for they do not know what they are doing." (Luke 23:34)

Then, one by one, I saw soldier after soldier, as they slowly began to lower their heads.

I wondered to myself, what are they thinking? Were any of them feeling any kind of remorse, or guilt?

Were any of them thinking, "Father, forgive us"?

Were any of them questioning, "How could this Man forgive

US after all the pain we have inflicted on His body?"

"How could He forgive US after we have humiliated Him the way we have?"

As if they had read my mind, I watched as one by one, most of the Roman soldiers turned and walked away, having completed their mission.

CHAPTER FORTY-SIX

Knowing the long, pain filled process that Jesus was facing, we all gathered around the cross as close as we could get.

Slowly, the chanting crowd dispersed.

There was nothing left to see.

I still could not take my eyes off Jesus. I determined in my mind that I would be there until His last breath.

Then, one of the criminals being crucified, taking in everything that was happening to Jesus, turned to Jesus with a big sneer on his face and said, *"So, You are the Christ, are You?"*

Jesus said nothing in return.

He continued, *"If You're able to save, which is what I have heard ... why don't You save Yourself? And while You're at it, You can save us with You!"*

I was just getting ready to give him a piece of my mind, when surprisingly it was the other criminal, hanging on the opposite cross, that came to the defense of Jesus.

"Don't you fear God?" the other thief asked. *"I do. Look at us, all three of us under the same condemnation. All three of us are going to die. But you and I ... we're getting our due reward! We are guilty of the crimes of which we have been accused, but this Man has done nothing wrong!"*

My heart melted within my chest as I listened to this criminal defending my Jesus.

Then the thought hit me. What did that thief just say? *"This Man has done nothing wrong?"*

Then I knew. This criminal must have been raised by a God-fearing mother! When he was young, he must have been taught right from wrong by his mother.

I turned and looked out into the small crowd that remained, checking to see if there were any family members of either of the thieves that were being crucified with Jesus. My heart broke, as I realized they were all alone.

I then turned to the small group of Jesus' supporters and asked, "Can you believe that this thief is defending Jesus?"

All attention was now on the man as he turned to Jesus and continued speaking. His voice shook with emotion, and tears ran down his face. *"Lord, will You please remember me when You come into Your kingdom?"*

Even though Jesus was in deep pain, I saw a slight smile come to His face.

Turning to the man, Jesus answered, "Assuredly I say unto you, today you will be with me in Paradise."
(Luke 23:39-43)

Once more I caught something the man said, that may have gone unnoticed by most of the crowd.

He just called Jesus, his 'Lord!'

I turned to point it out, but Maggie beat me to the punch.

"He just called Jesus his Lord, didn't he?"

How could something so lovely and beautiful happen right in the middle of such tragedy?

All of us that were gathered around felt a rush of peace and joy that completely took us by surprise, as a holy hush fell upon us.

Jesus had done it again!

How many times had we seen Him do this very thing ... **turn tragedy into triumph!**

Then it grew silent once more.

We watched as Jesus was now laboring to stay alive.

His lungs were filling with water from the great stress on his body.

Back and forth, He shifted His weight from His hands to His feet.

Each time He moved, He winced from the pain from the nails, that was like lightning striking through His hands and feet.

Then, focusing His attention on us, Jesus looked down at each one of us, acknowledging each one with a nod. All five of the Marys were there. John was there. Lazarus and Martha were there. Our new friend, Simon, was still there.

Then He slowly turned His head toward me and nodding His head toward John, He said softly, *"Woman, behold your son!"*

I quickly nodded back at Him, acknowledging His wish, and wrapped my arms tightly around John. I knew how much Jesus loved John. I wanted Jesus to know that I would take care of His close friend.

Then He focused His eyes on John and nodded His head

toward me and paused. *"Behold your mother!"* He stated, as tears spilled out of His eyes and fell down His blood-stained face.

Barely able to speak, John nodded, and with tears streaming down his weathered face as well, he replied, *"Don't worry about Your mother,"* as he squeezed my shoulders. *"I promise I'll take good care of her!"*

I saw a slight sense of relief in Jesus' eyes.

No one spoke for a couple of hours.

Around noon, there was a shift in the atmosphere. It was as if the sun was setting. It began growing darker and darker. (Matthew 27:45)

We began talking among ourselves as to what this might mean.

It was John that spoke up and said, "If you remember, one of the ten plagues that God caused to fall upon Egypt was the plague of darkness. Maybe that's what is happening here. Maybe God is allowing a plague to fall on us."

"Well, one thing is for certain," Mary the sister of Lazarus said, "I'm sure God is not happy with what is happening to Jesus!"

Then we sat quietly as it grew darker and darker, so as to not disturb Jesus.

Slowly, any strength that was left in Jesus' body, was being depleted not only by the weight of His body hanging on three nails, but it was also being depleted by the weight of the sin of the world that He was bearing.

Licking His parched and swollen lips, Jesus whispered as loudly as He could ... *"I thirst!"* (John 19:28)

A jar of sour wine was there near the crosses, along with a sponge on a long stick, to give to those on the cross.

A soldier, hearing what Jesus said, dipped the sponge in the wine and raised it to Jesus' lips. However, Jesus refused to drink from it.

His words were getting shorter and His voice weaker.

What could we say?

What could we do?

It was agonizing to sit there at the foot of the cross, and not be able to do anything to lessen the pain and suffering that Jesus was enduring.

At three o'clock in the afternoon a look of total anguish covered the face of Jesus and He surprised us all, when He suddenly cried out with a loud voice, "Eli, Eli, la-ma' sa-bach'-tha-ni!"

"What does that mean?" Maggie asked.

"It means, 'My God, My God, why hast Thou forsaken Me?'" John replied.

I didn't know what to think of that statement. Was God truly forsaking His Son, in the hour Jesus needed Him the most?

How could this be?

What could be the reasoning?

Like a flood, the scripture that Isaiah had written hundreds of years earlier came flooding into my mind.

He was led as a lamb to the slaughter.

I suddenly realized that every sin, from every person, from the past, to the present, to the future, was now resting on Jesus, as the sacrificial Lamb of God!

By taking on *all sin*, the Father, who cannot look upon sin, had to turn away from the sin that Jesus was willfully taking upon Himself, for the salvation and redemption of all mankind! (Habakkuk 1:13)

As the Apostle Paul would later write to the church in Corinth, "For He made Him who knew no sin to be sin for us, that we might become the righteousness of God in Him." (2 Corinthians 5:21)

Before our very eyes, we witnessed the weight of every horrendous sin that had ever been committed, or would ever be committed, now being thrust upon the body of Jesus!

We could all sense that it was *time*.

Every eye was on Him.

We watched as He gathered what little strength remained in His body, and as if it took everything within Him, He said, *"It is finished."* (John 19:30)

Then His head fell as He softly uttered His final words, *"Father, into Your hands I commit My spirit."* (Luke 23:46)

His body was quiet.

He had breathed His last breath.
Suddenly, there was another shift in the atmosphere.

With tears in my eyes, I turned to everyone around me and said, "Did you feel what I just felt?"

Every single one of us nodded our heads in agreement!

"He is here!" John exclaimed. "HE IS HERE!!!"

Maggie was the first one to ask. "WHO is here?"

"GOD!" John shouted.

John always seemed to have a great understanding of who God was ... who Jesus really was ... and who the Holy Spirit was.

"The presence of God, that has been restricted to the Holy of Holies ... HE IS HERE!"

We later found out that at 3 pm, the exact time Jesus took His last breath, the veil, that separated the Holy of Holies from the rest of the temple, had ripped asunder, from the top to the bottom. This meant that God was now among the people. This explained the sudden rush of God's presence we felt when Jesus died.

I was so conflicted.

On one hand I didn't want Jesus to die. But on the other hand, I was relieved that His suffering was over.

On one hand, I knew from scripture that He had just completed the mission that He was sent to do. But on the other hand, I honestly didn't care about His mission at this moment. All I wanted was to have my son back!
Then another revelation hit me. *"GOD WITH US!"*

I grabbed John by the arm and shouted, "You are so right, John! GOD IS WITH US!"

"That was the promise from Gabriel, when announcing the conception of Jesus. Gabriel said that His name would be called Emmanuel, meaning 'God with us.'"

And right when I thought it couldn't get any stranger, I turned, and to my amazement, standing there looking up at Jesus, was one of the Centurion Roman guards. He had the strangest look on his face.

He saw me looking at him.

He took a step toward me, but I held up my hand as if to tell him that I was not interested in anything he had to say.

He stopped and turned back toward the cross and looking up at Jesus he said with his voice filled with thick emotion, *"Truly, this Man was the Son of God!"* (Mark 15:39)

I felt my mouth drop open.

Did he just say what I thought he said?

As I took a step toward him, he turned to face me, and I saw tears welling up in his eyes.

"Excuse me. But did you just say what I think I heard you say? Did you just say that you now believe Jesus was the Son of God?"

"How could I not believe?" he replied, wiping away the tears with the back of his hand that were now flowing down his cheeks.

"But you believe that He is ... or was ... the Messiah?"

"Yes. I believe!"

We both turned and looked up at Jesus, hanging on the cross.

"So, what happens now?" he asked.

"To be honest with you … I don't know," I responded.

As strange as it may sound, I found myself wanting to hug one of the men responsible for driving the nails in the hands and feet of my Jesus.

I opened my arms to him.

I know it was an odd sight … me hugging this burly Roman Centurion guard … but it just felt right.

There in the shadow of the cross, two people that should have been enemies and at odds with each other … were united!

CHAPTER FORTY-SEVEN

I don't know how long we stood there, trying to decide what to do next.

The Roman guard that confessed that he was now a believer, had gone home.

The chanting crowd had long gone home.

A few of the Roman guards remained, waiting on the two thieves to die.

The only other people left were Simon of Cyrene, who had so wonderfully carried Jesus' cross, John, Lazarus, Martha, a few of the women that followed Jesus, and us *five Marys*.

It was John that broke the silence.

"Do you guys remember the time when Jesus got so upset in the temple, that He started kicking over tables?"

We all laughed.

"I heard He told them they had made the house of prayer into a den of thieves," Maggie stated.

"You heard correctly," John answered. "I had never seen Jesus so angry. He actually found a whip and used it to drive the money changers out of the temple!"

That opened the door.

We sat there at the foot of the cross, exchanging our "Jesus" stories for the next couple of hours.

Eventually Lazarus began telling his story about how Jesus had raised him from the dead.

Needless to say, there were a lot of questions asked about death, dying, and what awaits us after death!

As evening approached, we saw a stranger slowly walking toward us.

When he got close enough to see that it was Jesus hanging on the cross, we heard him exclaim loudly, "Oh no! It's true!"

"Sir, who are you, if you don't mind answering?" I asked.

"Oh, I am so sorry for interrupting. My name is Joseph. I'm from Arimathea. I have been a follower of Jesus for the past couple of years."

Each one of us greeted Joseph, introducing ourselves.

When I told him that I was Jesus' mother, he fell to his knees at my feet, taking my hands in his.

"Oh Mary! It is such a great honor to meet you. I am so very sorry for your great loss."

I pulled him to his feet and embraced him.

After bringing him up to speed on what had happened to Jesus, he asked, "So, have you decided what you are going to do with His body?"

"To be honest with you, we're not sure," I responded, looking to those around me for support.

"It would be my great honor to take care of His burial, if you don't mind?" Joseph stated. "I recently had a new tomb hewn out of rock nearby, that I would gladly give to you."

I shrugged my shoulders and said, "Sure. I don't have a problem with that."

"I'll be right back," he said, turning and running quickly in the direction of the city, "I'll go see if Pilate will give us permission."

I was so very grateful for Joseph. His kindness reminded me of my own Joseph. How I wished he was here ...

While we were waiting for Joseph to return, some of the Roman soldiers came to check and see if those on their crosses were still alive. The two thieves were, so we had to endure the cruelty of the soldiers, as they broke the legs of the two thieves. By breaking their legs, they could no longer shift their body weight between their hands and feet, and very quickly they both suffocated to death.

The only thing that made it bearable was knowing the one criminal that became a believer in Jesus would be with Jesus in paradise.

Paradise.

I stood there thinking about what Jesus had told the one thief. And I wondered if at that exact moment, they were already together in paradise?

Then the soldier approached Jesus.

"It looks like He's already dead," he said to no one in particular.

Mary, the sister of Lazarus, was kneeling at the foot of the cross. "He IS dead," she said, irritation showing in her voice. "No thanks to you ..."

"Sorry, I can't take your word for it. I have to make sure He's dead," the soldier responded.

Before any of us could react in time, he quickly thrust his spear into the side of Jesus!

Immediately Mary jumped to her feet, and shoved the soldier so hard he lost his balance and fell backwards, his head making a thumping sound when it hit the ground!

Lazarus came running over and got in between his sister and the soldier.

The soldier scrambled to his feet. "How dare you touch me? I could have you arrested!" he shouted into Mary's face.

"Please forgive her," Lazarus stated. "She was very close to Jesus. Please don't punish her!"

The tension on the soldier's face eased.

We all breathed a sigh of relief as he turned and walked away.

Then our attention was drawn back to Jesus.

Water and blood were flowing from the spear wound in His side. And another prophecy was fulfilled. This time it was the words of the prophet Zechariah, when he penned the words "Then they will look on Me whom they pierced". (Zachariah 12:10)

As we stood there watching the remainder of the blood and water flow from Jesus' side, Joseph came running back and joined us.

"Herod said it was okay for us to take His body and bury Him," he said, breathing heavy from his hasty trip.

Once more, after seeing how horribly the bodies of those crucified were treated, I was so very grateful to Joseph for his kindness.

Just as we prepared to lower the cross of Jesus, we saw another figure approaching.

He was also approaching us slowly, as if he was not sure if he would be welcomed or not.

He looked familiar.

Then I recognized him.

"You're Nicodemus, aren't you?" I asked.

"Yes," he responded. "And you're Mary, the mother of Jesus, correct?"

"Yes, I sure am."

"Were you a follower of Jesus?" I added.

Nicodemus grinned slightly.

"I guess I have been what you might call a 'secret' follower of Jesus," he responded.

"And what do you mean by that?" Maggie asked, stepping in with a look of concern on her face.

"You're a Pharisee, aren't you?" Maggie added, with a slight tone of accusation in her voice.

"Yes. You are correct," Nicodemus responded. "But I'm not like the other Pharisees."

"And just what is it, that makes you different than them?"

Maggie responded, taking a step aggressively toward him.

"I had an encounter with Jesus a while back that changed my life!" Nicodemus replied.

"Jesus made me realize that what my fellow Pharisee friends were accusing Him of was all wrong!" he continued.

"I'm still not sure I understand what He meant when He kept talking about 'being born again.' But He said one thing to me that was abundantly clear."

Maggie took another step closer. "And what was that?"

Nicodemus' eyes grew soft, and his voice clouded with emotion. "He told me that God so loved the world that He gave His only begotten Son, that whoever believes in Him should not perish but have everlasting life. He said that God did not send His Son into the world to condemn the world, but that the world through Him might be saved." (John 3:16-17)

Turning to Maggie, he said, "I admit that I was a coward. I admit I was afraid to be seen with Jesus."

Then he turned to all of us. "But He was so patient and kind with me."

Maggie finally smiled.

"So, you do believe that He *is* ... or *was* ... the Messiah ... the Son of God?"

"Oh yes!" Nicodemus replied. "I have no doubt that Jesus *IS* the Messiah!"

"That's why I am here," he continued. "When I heard that Jesus had been crucified, I thought the least I could do was bring some spices for His burial."

"Is that okay?" he added, turning and looking in my direction.

"Most certainly," I responded.

Then the five Marys and the other women watched, as John, Lazarus, Joseph, and Nicodemus slowly and tenderly lowered the cross to the ground.

I took the shawl from around my neck, and quickly covered His nakedness.

Even though I know that Jesus no longer felt any pain, it was difficult watching as John struggled to pull the nails from His hands and feet, without causing further damage.

We knew that we needed to get Jesus' body ready for burial quickly, because with it being a Friday, the Sabbath would go into effect at sundown. (John 19:31)

John's house was the closest, so the men carried the body of Jesus to his home to prepare His body for burial.

I asked everyone to step out of the room, so I could bath His body in private.

It was so quiet.

My mind went back to that silent night, thirty-three and a half years earlier. The night Jesus was born.

I remembered the first time I bathed His body as an infant. It was such a special time.

Now, here I was, bathing Him one last time.

His body was so horribly beaten and bruised, it took every ounce of strength I had, to complete the task before me.

He was literally covered in wounds, from the top of His head, to the soles of His feet. There were puncture marks in His brow from the crown of thorns, and lacerations on His face from being punched and slapped. The flesh on His back was so horribly shredded from the whip, I had to push parts of it back into place. As I washed His nail-pierced hands, I remembered how fascinated I was with His tiny fingers, right down to His fingernails, when He was born. As I washed His nail-pierced feet, I couldn't help but remember His first steps.

Memories flooded my mind.

Yes, it was difficult, but I would not have wanted it any other way.

When I finished bathing Him, I called Joseph, and the other four Marys into the room, and we gently wrapped His body in a shroud, covered His face with a special cloth, and tied His hands and feet with strips of cloth, according to Jewish custom. (John 19:40)

We then called Nicodemus and John into the room, and Nicodemus anointed Jesus with the spices he had brought with him.

Together, we then carried the body of Jesus to the new tomb.

I stood and wept, as the men rolled the heavy stone in place to seal the tomb.

Then, as difficult as it was, we turned and slowly walked back home.

Day One.

CHAPTER FORTY-EIGHT

Day Two.

"We're worried!"

Pilate looked up from some of the official documents he was reviewing.

Standing in front of him were several of the chief priests and Pharisees.

"We're worried that the disciples might steal His body."

"What in the world are you talking about?" Pilate asked, with a lack of patience showing in his voice.

"We're talking about Jesus!"

"Listen," Pilate answered, his voice now raising in agitation. "I let you talk me into having Him crucified, even though I found nothing wrong with Him. So, *what else do you want me to do?*" he asked, with contempt now in his voice.

"We've been thinking about Jesus saying that 'after three days I will rise again,' and we're worried that His disciples may steal His body, so they can claim He has been resurrected. If that happens, people may *really believe* that He has been raised from the dead!"

Turning back to the document in his hand, Pilate stated, without looking up, "if you're really that worried, you have my permission to take some guards with you, and secure the tomb so no one can open it. Now, get out of here and leave me alone!"

"There ... that should do it," the chief priest stated.

"Yeh, there's no way the disciples can move that stone now," one of the Pharisees agreed.

They stood there admiring the great job the soldiers had done of sealing the tomb.

"You," the chief priest stated, pointing to the biggest soldier of the bunch. "You stay here and stand guard over this tomb. And use as many guards as you need to make sure no one ... and I mean no one ... gets past you!"

"And that means all day and all night," one of the other Pharisees added.

They all nodded in agreement, patting each other on the back.

It was clear they were sure they had foiled any plan the disciples may have had to steal the body of Jesus.

"It would take an earthquake to move that stone now," one of them mumbled, as they turned and walked away with their haughty heads held high.

CHAPTER FORTY-NINE

Day two was agonizing for everyone that was a follower of Jesus.

First, there was the horrible news concerning Judas, and how he had taken his own life.

Second, ten of the eleven remaining disciples had failed Jesus. The only one that stayed with Jesus after He was arrested was John. The rest turned and ran away. Each one of them was trying to deal with the guilt they felt. They were so afraid that they too would be arrested, they stayed out of sight all day.

Peter was having nightmares about the rooster crowing. He was doubting himself so much he sneaked out and went fishing, even though it was the Sabbath.

With it being the Sabbath, Nicodemus and Joseph had returned to their homes, as had the five Marys, and John.

Normally, Mary, the mother of Jesus, would have worked around the house to keep her mind off of things that troubled her, but it was the Sabbath. So, all she could do was sit around the house with Maggie and talk about all the "what ifs."

CHAPTER FIFTY

Matthew 28:1 Now after the Sabbath, as the first day of the week began to dawn, Mary Magdalene and the other Mary came to see the tomb.

Mark 16:1 Now when the Sabbath was past, Mary Magdalene, Mary the mother of James, and Salome bought spices, that they might come and anoint Him.

Luke 24:8 And they remembered His words. 9 Then they returned from the tomb and told all these things to the eleven and to all the rest. 10 It was Mary Magdalene, Joanna, Mary the mother of James, and the other women with them, who told these things to the apostles.

Day Three.

"Are you coming with us?" Maggie asked.

"I don't know," I responded. "Who all is going?"

"Me, and Mary, Lazarus' sister, Mary, the mother of James and Joses, the other Mary, and Joanna."

I couldn't help but smile.

"So, every Mary except me!"

Maggie smiled in return. "Yes, every Mary except you!"

I had to admit I was having a difficult time with the death of Jesus.

"Thanks, Maggie. But I think I'll let you guys go early this morning, and I'll go a little later. I kind of want to be there by myself. Is that okay?"

"Are you sure? We have some wonderful spices we're taking, in case we're able to anoint His body."

"Sorry. But I'm not feeling up to it. Okay?"

Maggie gave me a big hug.

"Of course, that's okay. I'm sure the other Marys and Joanna won't mind a bit."

As she headed out the door she turned and asked over her shoulder, "Is there anything you need at the market? I can stop by before I head back home."

"No," I told her. "I think I have enough for the next few days. But thanks!"

It was still dark outside, so I decided to lay back down for a few minutes. Sleep, the last two nights, had been difficult to come by. I couldn't get the image of Jesus' mutilated body out of my dreams.

CHAPTER FIFTY-ONE

I had just drifted off to sleep when my bed began to shake.

I jumped up out bed and ran to the window, looking outside in the darkness, trying to get my bearings.

I finally realized it was an earthquake.

At that exact moment Maggie, the other three Marys, and Joanna were slowly making their way through the dark streets, on their way to the tomb, when the ground beneath them began to quake as well.

"What is that?" Maggie asked, with a tremor in her voice.

"Oh, that's just another earthquake," Joanna stated, trying to act like it was no big deal. "Don't you remember the one that happened three days ago?"

They all stopped walking, waiting for the ground beneath their feet to settle back down.

Mary, the sister of Lazarus, trying to make light of the situation, replied, "Yeh, if you all remember, something spectacular happened during that last earthquake. Jesus died, and at that exact moment the veil in the temple was ripped apart!"

"That's right," they all agreed in unison. "That was awesome!"

Little did they know, but something spectacular was happening again!

At that exact moment, two angels were appearing at the

tomb while the earth was shaking, and they began rolling the stone away from the entrance.

Their appearance was like lightning, and their clothes were white as snow.

The soldiers that were guarding were so petrified they began quaking in their boots, and passed out, falling down like dead men!

Also, at that exact moment, the blood in the body of Jesus, that had been coagulated for three days, began to turn liquid again! The heart of Jesus, that had stopped beating three days earlier, began beating again. The lungs of Jesus, that stopped breathing three days earlier, began to fill with oxygen again, and His cold lifeless body began growing warmer and warmer!

Suddenly, His eyes opened, and His fingers began moving, and His legs began twitching!

Then HE SAT UP!

ALIVE!

FOREVERMORE!!!

He removed the burial cloth wrapped around His head, folded it, and laid it aside.

He then removed the linen shroud, and laid it aside as well.

Then, the same way the veil was ripped asunder, during the earthquake three days earlier, allowing all to enter the Holy of Holies, the stone blocking the tomb was completely rolled out of the way by the angels, allowing Jesus to walk away from death, hell, and the grave ... **VICTORIOUS!**

So, when Maggie and her friends arrived at the tomb, they were met with quite a surprise.

First, laying on the ground, unconscious, were the two soldiers that were supposed to be guarding the tomb.

Second, the stone that was supposed to be in front of the tomb had been rolled away.

And third, there were two angels sitting on top of the stone!

"Don't be afraid," one of the angels said, "I know that you are looking for Jesus, who was crucified. But He is not here. He has risen, just like He said He would."

The women could barely hold their composure.

The angel continued, "Do you want to come inside and see where He lay?"

Slowly, they approached the tomb, each one trying to push the other in front of her.

Maggie was the first one with enough courage to stick her head inside the tomb.

Turning around she shouted to the other women, "He's right! Jesus is NOT HERE!"

"Why do you seek the living among the dead?" the other angel asked. "Don't you remember what He told you while He was with you in Galilee?"

The women looked at one another, with no one willing to answer.

"He told you," the angel continued, "how 'the Son of Man must be delivered into the hands of sinful men, and be crucified, and the third day rise again.'" (Luke 24:7)

"He's right," Maggie shouted. "Now I remember exactly what you are talking about!"

"Now go quickly," the angel continued. "Go and tell His disciples that He is risen from the dead, and indeed He is going before you into Galilee. There you will see Him. Behold, I have told you." (Matthew 28:7)

The women took off as fast as they could go. They were afraid, yet they were filled with great joy!

Suddenly, there in the road in front of them stood Jesus!!!!

They could not believe their eyes!

"Rejoice!" Jesus said to them, His face radiant and full of joy.

Immediately they fell at His feet, and worshipped Him.

"Don't be afraid," Jesus said to them. "Get up and go tell My brethren to go to Galilee. There they will see Me."

Bursting through the door of the room where the disciples were hiding, the women tried to tell them what the angel had told them, and what Jesus Himself, had told them.

Most of the disciples doubted what they were saying, however; Peter and John decided to go check it out.

It was comical seeing two grown men act like young boys as they almost knocked each other down, racing toward the tomb.

John outran Peter and got to the tomb first. He leaned over, looked inside and saw the linen shroud laying there, with the burial cloth folded in a separate place, but was too afraid to go inside.

However, when Peter reached the tomb, he didn't hesitate at all. He boldly walked right into the tomb.

All doubt about what had happened to Jesus left Peter and John immediately.

They quickly returned and told the rest of the disciples what they had seen.

"Now what should we do?" Peter asked.

"I think we should do what Jesus said for us to do," John answered. "Let's go to Galilee and wait for Him to show up."

And show up He did!!!

The disciples were still afraid of what the Jews and Pharisees might do, so they locked the doors of the room where they were hiding.

Suddenly, there He was!

He didn't knock on the door. He didn't open the door. He simply APPEARED before them!

"Peace be with you!" He exclaimed.

However, His sudden appearance caught them off guard.

He could see they were still struggling with the reality of what was happening right before their very eyes, so He held out His hands and showed them the nail prints in His hands. Then, He raised His robe, and showed them the scar in His side.

All doubt was gone!

Everyone except Thomas, who wasn't there at the time, knew that without a doubt Jesus had indeed been raised from the dead, just like He said He would!

Later, when the disciples told Thomas about Jesus, he simply could not bring himself to believe what they were saying.

"Unless I see the nail prints in His hands and put my finger into His side, I will not believe it," he said.

A week later, Jesus appeared to them again. Again, the door was locked, but Jesus just *appeared*, and gave them the same greeting, *"Peace be with you!"*

This time Thomas was there. He was awe struck as Jesus wasn't there one second, but was there the next!

Thomas just stood there with his mouth hanging wide open.

With a slight grin on His face, Jesus approached Thomas.

"Here Thomas," He said. "Put your finger here in the nail prints in My hands. Reach out your hand and thrust it into My side. Stop doubting and believe!"

Falling to his knees, Thomas shouted out, "My Lord and My God!"

CHAPTER FIFTY-TWO

I was sound asleep when Maggie came bursting through my bedroom door, shouting, "HE'S ALIVE! HE'S ALIVE!"

"What?" I shouted back at her. "What are you talking about?"

I was rubbing the sleep from my eyes, and trying to figure out what was happening.

Maggie was so excited she was about to hyperventilate!

"He's alive … Jesus is alive!" she finally stated.

Now it was my turn to hyperventilate.

"Are you sure?"

"Oh yes! I saw Him with my own eyes!"

"And He was alive … and talking?"

"Oh yes! Very much alive and talking. And walking! He is RESURRECTED FROM THE DEAD, Mary!"

I knew that Jesus had talked about being resurrected, but I was too afraid to allow myself to believe it.

"Where is He?" I asked.

"He is meeting with the disciples in Galilee this evening."

"Did He say anything about meeting with me?"

Surely, He would want to meet with me, I thought.

I could see that Maggie wished He had said something about meeting with me.

"I'm sorry, Mary. But He only said He would meet with the disciples."

"That's okay," I told her. "I'm sure He will show up sooner or later."

The next few days were quite interesting.

The Pharisees were spreading a lie that the disciples had stolen the body of Jesus.

People began believing the lie, but then Jesus started showing up in different places.

He appeared to the disciples three different times.

He appeared to the apostles.

He also appeared to over five hundred of His followers at the same time.

Then, one day James, my son, was at my house. He, Maggie and I were reminiscing about the times and things Jesus said and did.

Suddenly, there He was!

Yes, He appeared to me!!!

CHAPTER FIFTY-THREE

I thought they were going to break my door down they were beating on it so hard.

When I opened the door, there stood Mary, the sister of Lazarus, Mary, the mother of James and Joses, and the other Mary.

Maggie, hearing the commotion came running into the living room.

"What's going on?" she asked, with a big smile on her face, seeing that all five Marys were together again.

The other Mary surprised everyone by speaking up. "He's gone!" she blurted out.

"Who's gone?" Maggie asked.

"Jesus. Jesus is gone!"

My first thought was that the Pharisees had found Him and killed Him again.

Seeing the panic on my face, the other Mary quickly spoke again.

"No! Not that way! He's okay, but He is *gone* ..."

Relief filled my mind.

"So, where has He gone?" I asked.

"To heaven!" she blurted out again.

"What???" I asked.

Mary of Bethany stepped up and answered. "He met with the disciples near Bethany, and they said He gave them some final instructions about taking His message to the whole world. Then they watched Him as He ascended up into heaven."

Everyone was watching, to see how I would react.

I smiled.

"Home ..." I said softly.

They all looked at me with a puzzled look.

Quietly Maggie asked, *"Home???"*

"Yes. *Home*," I repeated. "He is now home with His Father!"

Suddenly, tears filled my eyes.

The magnitude of what I said began to sink in.

"Yes," Maggie said softly, as tears also filled her eyes. "He is home, isn't He?"

It was wonderful having all five Marys together for such a tender moment as this.

"I was so blessed to be His mother for the past thirty-three years," I continued. "But it *was* time for Him to go back to His Father!"

"So ... now what?" Maggie asked. "What are we supposed to do now?"

"That's why we are here," the other Mary said, with the rest of the Marys nodding in approval. "When Jesus left, He told the disciples that we were to go to Jerusalem, and wait there until we received power from on high. We stopped to get you and Maggie to go with us."

"Power from on high?" Maggie asked. "What in the world does that mean?"

Everyone looked at each other and we all shrugged our shoulders.

"Sounds like we're going to find out," Maggie stated, leading the five Marys out the door and down the street.

CHAPTER FIFTY-FOUR

Looking Luke in the eyes I asked him, "Okay, what exactly did Jesus say for us to do?"

"He told us not to depart from Jerusalem," Luke responded, "but instead, to wait for the Promise of the Father, which we heard from Him. He said something about how John truly baptized with water, but He said that we were going to be baptized with the Holy Spirit."

"Do you have any idea what He meant?" Luke continued.

Before I could respond, John stepped up and said, "I think I do. Do you remember on the last day of the feast, when Jesus stood up and started talking about how if anyone thirsts, let him come to Him and drink? He said whoever believes in Him, as the Scripture has said, out of his heart will flow rivers of living water."

"Yes, I do remember that." Luke answered.

"I think we are getting ready to experience what He was talking about," John continued. "I think that if we just do what Jesus told us to do, and believe what He told us, I think we are going to be baptized with the Holy Spirit."

"What is that going to look like?" I asked.

"Here is what Jesus told us the other day," Luke answered. "He said that we would receive power when the Holy Spirit has come upon us. He also said that we would be witnesses about Him, in Jerusalem, and in all Judea and Samaria, and to the end of the earth."

"All we have to do is wait?" I asked.

Luke shook his head. "That's the way I understood it."

More and more people continued making their way into the upper room.

"How many more are going to show up?" I thought to myself.

All of the disciples, Nicodemus, Joseph of Arimathea, Lazarus and Martha showed up. The lame man that was healed at the pool of Bethesda, showed up. The young man that Jesus raised from the dead, showed up, along with his mother. Several of those that were healed of leprosy showed up. The blind man that Jesus used spit and mud to heal his blindness showed up. The man that was mute and deaf and Jesus stuck His fingers in his ears, then spit and touched his tongue, showed up.

I recognized people that had been there when Jesus fed the thousands.

But my heart almost skipped a beat when all four of Jesus' brothers came walking in!

"What are you guys doing here?" I shouted at them.

Smiling, Joseph gave me a big hug and responded, "Hi Mom! We heard about the *Promise* that Jesus made. You don't think we would miss out on this, do you?"

The other four Marys, the disciples, and now my sons. My heart was full and overflowing already!

"Alright everyone!" Peter shouted out, getting everyone's attention. "I'm sure everyone is wondering what we are doing here."

"Here is all I know," Peter continued. "We are doing what Jesus told us to do. How many times did He challenge us in the last three years, concerning things we didn't understand? But every single time we did what He told us to do, we ended up seeing something amazing."

I watched as each and every head began nodding.

"Nathanael, did you understand, after the resurrection, when Jesus appeared to us while we were fishing, and He told us to cast our net on the other side of the boat?"

"Not at all!" Nathanael responded, a huge smile appearing on his face. "I wanted to tell Him that He should leave fishing to the professional fishermen."

"But what did we do?" Peter asked.

Smiling even bigger, Nathanael replied, "We DID what He told us to DO!"

"And how did that work out?"

Nathanael was now laughing out loud. "We saw something mind blowing. We went from catching absolutely nothing, to catching so many fish I thought it was going to break the nets! We counted the fish. There were one hundred and fifty-three of the biggest fish we ever caught!"

"So, what are we going to do?" Peter asked, looking around at everyone.

One hundred and twenty people all shouted in unison, *"DO WHAT HE TOLD US TO DO!"*

One day turned into two, and still we continued waiting and praying.

Three days turned into four. Four days turned into five, and then six and seven.

I honestly thought some may get tired of waiting, and leave. But, they didn't.

We prayed. We worshipped. We read from the holy scriptures.

On the tenth day John shouted out to everyone, "Do you guys know what today is?"

Everyone just stared at him for a few seconds, then Luke shouted out, "I do! Today is the Day of Pentecost!"

Luke was right! It had been fifty days since the day Jesus was resurrected, and ten days since He ascended back into heaven.

No sooner had Luke made that declaration and suddenly out of nowhere a sound like that of a rushing mighty wind from heaven filled the entire room where we were sitting.

Ruach!

I knew in an instant what was happening.

Ruach!

I remembered my dad using that exact word when he told our family how God *breathed life* into Adam in the beginning!

That was what was happening. God was actually *breathing* new life into us!

Even though the doors and windows were closed, a heavenly wind blew over me so strong I felt it blow the hair away from my face!

All I remember is raising my hands in praise and worship, and suddenly it felt like the top of my head was on fire!

I looked around, and I saw what actually appeared to be tongues of fire resting on every person in the room!

Then, just when I thought it couldn't get any stranger, it did!

I began hearing different languages being spoken. All around me, I witnessed common people starting to speak in a language I knew they did not know!

Then it happened to me! The praises that I had been offering up to God in Hebrew had suddenly changed into a foreign language. And it happened to be a language that I had heard on the streets from foreigners in the city that were there to celebrate the Passover!

I knew what it was ... it was *Ruach* ... the wind from God that I heard my dad speak about when talking about the Holy of Holies.

As the wind of *Ruach* filled the room, everyone began speaking in other tongues!

Looking back on it, it was rather comical. All one hundred and twenty of us were trying to praise God in Hebrew and Greek, yet what came out was a foreign language to us.

The joy of the Lord was filling us up, inside and out!

Then, being filled with the Holy Spirit, all one hundred and twenty of us went bursting out of the upper room onto the street, still speaking in other tongues.

Have you heard the expression, *in the right place at the right time?*

That is exactly what happened. God had drawn devout Jews from fifteen different countries right outside the upper room.

Hearing the commotion coming from the upper room, they gathered closer and closer, so they were there as witnesses as we spilled out into the streets.

There were Parthians and Medes and Elamites, those dwelling in Mesopotamia, Judea and Cappadocia, Pontus and Asia, Phrygia and Pamphylia, Egypt and the parts of Libya adjoining Cyrene, along with visitors from Rome, both Jews and proselytes, and Cretans and Arabs.

And each one heard someone speaking their home language and were completely astounded!

When I finally stopped speaking the language I was speaking, I opened my eyes to see a young man from Asia staring at me face to face!

With a quizzical look on his face, he leaned in and asked, "Aren't you from right here in Galilee?"

Not knowing where this conversation was going, I answered with a questioning, "Yesss …?"

"Have you spent time in Asia?"

Again, I answered with a question in my voice … "No …?"

"Then where did you learn how to speak Mandarin?"

"Is that the language I was speaking?"

"Yes. How did you learn that language?"

Before I could answer he pointed at Bartholomew, and asked, "And where did he learn Mandarin?"

Bartholomew was oblivious that we were talking about

him. He just kept on praising God in a language he knew nothing about.

I just smiled at the young man and answered, "All I can tell you is that it is a gift from God."

"What was I saying, if you don't mind telling me?" I asked the young man.

"You were giving praise and glory to Almighty God!!!" he replied.

I looked around, and saw this same conversation being repeated with a lot of the foreigners.

I also heard the same question, "What does this mean?" being repeated over and over.

I knew the answer to that question. I knew why we were speaking languages we didn't know. We were being witnesses to people in Jerusalem, Judea, Samaria, and to the end of the earth just like Jesus said we would.

However, some of those that were skeptical about what was happening started making fun of us and saying, *"They're just drunk on some kind of new wine!"*

Realizing that someone needed to speak up and explain what just happened, Peter gathered the eleven around him, and climbed up on a nearby wall, and as loudly as he could speak, began explaining what they were witnessing.

"Men of Judea and all who dwell in Jerusalem, let this be known to you, and heed my words. These people are not drunk, as you suppose, since it is only nine am in the morning."

"What you are witnessing is the fulfillment of the prophecy that was written by the prophet Joel. As Jews, you should know what Joel wrote."

One of the men standing near Peter shouted out, "So, what did Joel say about all of this?"

Peter smiled, "He said, 'And it shall come to pass in the last days, says God, that I will pour out My Spirit on all flesh. Your sons and your daughters shall prophesy, your young men shall see visions, and your old men shall dream dreams.'"

Peter could see that he had everyone's attention, so he continued on. "Joel also said, 'And on My men servants and on My maid servants I will pour out My Spirit in those days, and they shall prophesy.

"'I will show wonders in heaven above and signs in the earth beneath, such as blood and fire and vapor of smoke.

"'The sun shall be turned into darkness, and the moon into blood, before the coming of the great and awesome day of the Lord.'"

Still skeptical, the man in the front of the crowd shouted out once more, "And when will these things happen?"

Peter paused, and asked, "Were any of you in Jerusalem fifty days ago?"

Several raised their hands.

"Do you remember how dark it got at noon that day?" Peter asked.

The man asking all of the question responded, "Yeah, I was in Jerusalem for the Passover, and yes, I remember how it suddenly turned dark in the middle of the day."

Peter smiled at him. "And, do you remember what was

happening at Mount Calvary when it turned dark?"

The man was now quiet.

"I'll tell you what was happening," Peter said. "Jesus Christ was being crucified."

Continuing on, Peter returned to the words of Joel. "Joel said that it shall come to pass that whoever calls on the name of the Lord shall be saved."

The man in the front was now intrigued, and asked Peter, "Can you tell us more about this Jesus fellow?"

"Absolutely," Peter responded.

"Men of Israel, pay attention to what I am getting ready to tell you about Jesus of Nazareth. He was a Man attested by God to you by miracles, wonders, and signs which God did through Him in your midst, as you yourselves also know. Him, being delivered by the determined purpose and foreknowledge of God, you Jews have taken by lawless hands, have crucified, and put Him to death. However, God raised Him up, having loosed the pains of death, because it was not possible that He should be held by it."

"For David says concerning Him, 'I foresaw the Lord always before my face, for He is at my right hand, that I may not be shaken. Therefore, my heart rejoiced, and my tongue was glad, moreover my flesh also will rest in hope.

"For You will not leave my soul in Hades, nor will You allow Your Holy One to see corruption. You have made known to me the ways of life, and You will make me full of joy in Your presence.'"

I looked around, and every person around us was completely focused on what Peter was saying.

"Men and brethren, let me speak freely to you about the patriarch David, that is both dead and buried, and his tomb is with us to this day. Therefore, being a prophet, and knowing that God had sworn with an oath to him that of the fruit of his body, according to the flesh, He would raise up the Christ to sit on his throne, he, foreseeing this, spoke concerning the resurrection of the Christ, that His soul was not left in Hades, nor did His flesh see corruption."

Long gone was the disrespect in the man's voice with all the questions.

"So, this is the *Jesus* we have heard about that was crucified?"

"Yes," Peter responded. "This Jesus God has raised up, of which we are all witnesses."

Peter paused, and asked, "How many here saw Jesus after He was resurrected from the dead?"

At least one hundred of those that were in the upper room raised their hands.

Peter continued, "Therefore being exalted to the right hand of God, and having received from the Father the promise of the Holy Spirit, He poured out this which you now see and hear."

I looked around and saw that Peter was not only speaking to the crowd of people that had gathered, he was also speaking to those of us that were in the upper room.

Maggie pulled me close and whispered loudly, *"So, what just happened to us was the promise concerning the Holy Spirit that Jesus talked about?"*

I shook my head *yes*, and whispered back to her. *"Be quiet*

Maggie, I don't think Peter is finished."

As if on cue, Peter continued, "For David did not ascend into the heavens, but he says himself, 'the Lord said to my Lord, sit at My right hand, until I make Your enemies Your footstool.

"'Therefore, let all the house of Israel know assuredly that God has made this Jesus, whom you crucified, both Lord and Christ!'"

Now when those that stood by heard this, they were cut to the heart, and said to Peter and the rest of the apostles, "Men and brethren, what shall we do?"

Then Peter said to them, "Repent, and let every one of you be baptized in the name of Jesus Christ for the remission of sins, and you shall receive the gift of the Holy Spirit. For the promise is to you and to your children, and to all who are afar off, as many as the Lord our God will call."
(All scriptures referenced are found in Acts 1 & 2)

CHAPTER FIFTY-FIVE

What happened next was amazing.

Those that witnessed what happened to us in the upper room and heard Peter's sermon, went out and began gathering people together. By the end of the day around three thousand people believed what Peter preached and were saved!

Many signs and wonders were being done by the apostles, and there was great unity among all of the believers and followers of Jesus.

A few days later, another five thousand were saved.

As more and more people became believers in Jesus, it made His horrible death easier for me to bear.

This was what He came for!
This was what He was beaten for!
This was why He had to die!

CHAPTER FIFTY-SIX

There were numerous times all five of us Marys would get together and reminisce about the times we spent with Jesus.

We formed a sisterhood that carried us through many of the challenges that the church faced the first several years after the Day of Pentecost.

Each Mary had her own unique experience with Jesus.

Rightfully so, my experience as His mother, was more intimate than the rest of the Marys. I was there for His first breath in the stable in Bethlehem, and I was there when He took His last breath on the cross.

I was there to change His diapers and feed Him as an infant. I was there for the challenges of those teenage years, and I was there as He entered adulthood.

I was the one that pushed Him to perform His first miracle, and I was there for the fulfillment of His promise to send the Holy Spirit.

Mary Magdalene's experience with Jesus was unique in that she was the only Mary that was delivered from the very pit of hell. She knew what it was like to go from extreme darkness, into the marvelous light of His love and salvation.

Mary, the mother of James and Joses, had an experience with Jesus that started when He called her two sons to be His disciples. However, as she began to follow Jesus because of her sons, she came to know Jesus for herself.

Mary, the sister of Lazarus, was the first Mary to see the

resurrection power of Jesus! Her faith was challenged, during the four-day wait, but in the end, she got to see a miracle of monumental proportions!

Even though the other Mary was the last Mary to show up in Jesus' ministry, she was faithful to stay at the cross until the very end!

Yes, each Mary had different experiences with Jesus. However, we all had one common experience. We all experienced the love of Jesus Christ!

A week before the one-year anniversary of our upper room experience, I sent out invitations to everyone that was there that day when the Holy Ghost was poured out on us all in such a powerful way, and I invited everyone to meet once more on the Day of Pentecost in the upper room.

It was a glorious day to be reunited with such wonderful believers. But it was also a sad day because there were several believers that for sake of the gospel had already become martyrs, such as Steven.

However, we realized that we were part of a spiritual movement, that was going to change the world!

EPILOGUE

Were there challenges for each Mary that became a follower of Jesus?

Most certainly!

But there were also great rewards.

When Nicodemus showed up with spices to anoint Jesus the day Jesus was crucified, he and Mary, the sister of Lazarus, started a courtship that ended up with them getting married. They now have four children. Needless to say, Uncle Lazarus loves telling the children about his resurrection story!

James and Joses made Mary, their mother, proud when they stepped up and became leaders in the church in Jerusalem.

The experience of being there for the death, burial, and resurrection of Jesus changed the "other" Mary in a way none of us expected. She went from being shy and quiet, to a powerful witness for the cause of Christ. She ended up moving to Rome to help in the church that the Apostle Paul started there. In Paul's letter to the church in Rome, he mentions her by name! (Romans 16:6)

And, Mary Magdalene (Maggie) ended up becoming my daughter-in-law, when she married my second youngest son, Simon. They are leaders in the church in Jerusalem. I can't wait for them to give me grandchildren!

The End

Acknowledgements

All glory be to God and our Lord
and Savior Jesus Christ.

Judy Swindle:
Thank you for being a great "big" sister. You are an inspiration to everyone around you and a wonderful role model. Thank you so much for your editing skills, suggestions, and correcting me when I went "comma crazy."

Crystal Deeds:
Thank you for being a wonderful friend. Thank you for your editing skills and immense help in self-publishing.

Jim Shain:
You have helped edit most of my books, including this one, for which I am most grateful.

Jennifer Upchurch:
My wife, my partner in life, my partner in ministry, my love, and my best friend.

My Children:
Heather Upchurch Roesch and husband, Jason.
Kyle Steven Upchurch.
Zachary Alan Brandt.

My Grandchildren:
Jaylyn Alyssa Roesch
Addylyn Marie Roesch.

My Siblings:
Judy & William (Randy) Swindle
Roy & Kathy Upchurch,
Fay & Albert (OJ) Suarez
Bill & Joy Rutherford,
Melody & Fred Albanito.

My In-laws:
Jess & Mary Childers

In Memory of my parents:
Charles & Mildred Upchurch

Other Books by Steve E. Upchurch

The Adventures of Matthew & Andy:

In this series of children's books, Matthew, a ten-year-old boy, has started reading his Bible but he is struggling to understand what he is reading. So, he prays and asks God to help him. God sends a very unique angel named Andy in Matthew's dreams to start taking him back in time to see first-hand how exciting the stories in the Bible can be.

Each Bible adventure is described with its exciting twists and turns as seen through the eyes of ten-year-old Matthew, with his quirky sidekick.

The Adventures of Matthew & Andy: Genesis
The Adventures of Matthew & Andy: Exodus - Joshua
The Adventures of Matthew & Andy: Judges - 2 Samuel

Bartholomew And The Christ Child:

This fictitious story is about a fifteen-year-old boy named Bartholomew whose family owned the Bethlehem Inn, and how their encounter with Jesus as the Christ Child, born in their stable changed their lives.